Corpse at the National Gallery

A Dupree Sisters Mystery

by

Allen B. Boyer

For information, email Cozy Cat Press, cozycatpress@aol.com or visit our website at: www.cozycatpress.com

COZY CAT
P R E S S

Cover photo: View of the Kogod Courtyard at the Smithsonian American Art Museum and National Portrait Gallery, December 28, 2012, 06:21 a.m. by Zack Frank

ISBN: 978-1-946063-90-8
Printed in the United States of America

Dedication: For David Pegher, an artist, father, and husband gone too soon.

Chapter 1: A Sense of Urgency

His shoes smacked loudly on the granite floor as he ran. The sound cracked out a rhythm that cast a sense of urgency throughout the empty halls of the National Portrait Gallery in Washington D.C. The man was breathing hard with each stride. At his age, running was not something he did very often. However, this was no ordinary situation.

He stopped when he reached the entrance to the Kogod Courtyard, a large enclosed space where a hundred people were seated, enjoying a catered dinner prepared by one of Washington's best chefs. Catching his breath, the man looked around at the faces before him, noting the conversations and laughter that seemed to occupy every table.

He lingered at the entrance to the courtyard, knowing he was about to say something that would change the evening's festivities for everyone in the room. In fact, he guessed it would even change the fortunes of most every politician in Washington, D.C. His announcement might even make the top story on the evening news, or so he thought. There were many ripples he was about to cast with just a few well-chosen words. The effects of those words gave him a feeling of self-importance. A slight smile peeked out briefly between his cheeks as he pondered the power in the words he was about to utter. He wiped a thin layer of sweat from his forehead with the back of his hand. He adjusted his suit coat, straightened his tie and took a deep breath before stepping into the courtyard.

For the first few seconds, it appeared the crowd was oblivious to his appearance. He stood in front of a band playing soft dinner music, unsure of what to do next. He scanned the crowd before finding one face, sitting at a table closest to him, who glanced in his direction. It was a familiar face. An old acquaintance who quickly offered a friendly smile upon making eye contact. The man did not reciprocate the warm expression from his friend. Instead, he broke eye contact and scanned the rest of the room again.

He cleared his throat and pondered his words one more time. He took one final measured step towards the affluent crowd attending this gala. He waited for the band to finish their musical rendition of Frank Sinatra's *The Way You Look Tonight*. Once the music stopped, the only sounds filling the air were polite conversations and utensils gently tapping on dishes.

At first, the man tried to speak in a normal tone of voice, but no one paid attention to him. His delicate voice was simply too weak to hear. He paused, nervously ran one hand through his short white hair, then waved both hands at the crowd in a furious attempt to gain their attention.

With the loudest voice he could muster he yelled something that caused every face sitting around the tables closest to him to stop eating and turn in his direction. He yelled the same words even louder. Again, more tables paused from their meal and more eyes turned in his direction. He yelled the same message for a third time at the top of his lungs. People seated towards the back of the room now stopped eating and, judging by the expressions on their faces, were listening to what he said.

He scanned the room. No one was eating. The band was silent. Every eye in the room was locked on him. It was clear that the words he chose to use were enough to make an impression on every person in the room. They were words that conveyed a sense of gravity. Words that were so powerful he knew no one would forget him, or this night, for the rest of their lives.

Chapter 2: Three Weeks Later

Inside a narrow red-bricked home across from Lafayette Square, two curious cats lead a life of leisure. It is a home where the cats have free reign to roam where they wish when they wish. Most mornings the cats enjoy lounging on the floor of a spacious sitting room on the main floor. It is the only room in the house where the morning sun creates warm round patches of light for the cats to enjoy. However, there is one day, a Sunday, that the cats do not choose to lounge in the sunlight. Instead, they ignore the sunshine to follow their curious instincts. Curiosity that leads them to watch their owners behave in a rather unusual manner.

It is on Sundays that Mezzo and Oliver become observers. Instead of occupying the sitting room, they linger in the downstairs hallway to watch their owners scurry around the house. Usually, it's the two cats who like to run from room to room with reckless abandon. However, the cats were beginning to notice that on this one day out of the week the roles were reversed. Their owners were the ones who became quite loud and quite busy.

When this particular day arrived, the cats quietly observed how their owners moved from room to room with hurried steps. They saw them do this over and over again, moving between the kitchen and the back room, which was rather strange. They also noted how their owners' voices grew louder and sharper while they scurried between both rooms. To explain such a behavior, Mezzo and Oliver's instincts told them that the Dupree sisters must be chasing a very elusive mouse. However, after repeated investigations around the house the cats quickly determined their instincts were wrong. No mouse was found. So they remained seated in the hallway, watching and listening to the activity before them.

"Grab the chips, Ruth!" one sister called out from the kitchen.

"I have the chips. Grab the dip, Charlotte!" the other sister replied from the kitchen.

Mezzo and Oliver remained seated on the hardwood floor of the downstairs hall, their heads turning from side to side while they observed the activity. They watched Ruth Dupree linger in the back room to set up two small tables in front of the TV. They spotted the older sister, Charlotte Dupree, carrying two bowls of food in from the kitchen and place them on the tables. Mezzo, always the curious one, hopped up on the couch and sniffed around one bowl before being gently pushed away by the back of Charlotte's hand. An oddly shaped ball was placed on the couch next to Ruth, who quickly placed it on her lap. Finally, it appeared both sisters were settled on the couch.

"Rub it for good luck, Charlotte!" Ruth instructed before picking up the football and holding it in front of her sister.

"I know the routine," Charlotte grumbled before reaching over and petting the surface of the ball as if it were one of their cats. "It's not the first time I've watched a Washington Redskins football game with you, Ruth."

"But this is an important game," Ruth observed before scooping a few chips from one bowl and popping them into her mouth. "You know as well as I do that today's winner will be in first place. This late in the season…it's an important game for our team to win.

We must support the team, sister. We *must* do everything lucky to help them win."

Charlotte also snatched a chip from the bowl and slipped it in her mouth. Ruth cracked open a small container of dip and placed it on a side table. Charlotte stood up and stepped into the kitchen before returning with two glasses of iced tea. She handed one to Ruth, who was opening a small bag of baby carrots and a second container of dip. Ruth again turned to her lucky football and rubbed it with great vigor.

"Magic of George Allen," she begged, "please be with our team today."

Ruth stopped rubbing the ball, picked it up with one hand and held it high in the air like it was some kind of trophy.

"Do you remember when we got this?" she asked, grinning at the ball.

"Of course," Charlotte replied. "We outbid other people at a fundraiser for it years ago. Coach Allen even signed it and wrote a very nice letter explaining that it was a football they used in Super Bowl VII against the Miami Dolphins. I always liked Coach Allen. He was such a nice man. How much did we pay for it?"

"I don't recall the price," Ruth mumbled, eyes fixed on the ball. "I just know they scored their only touchdown in the Super Bowl with this ball, or so Coach Allen told us."

"Such a nice man," Charlotte murmured to herself.

Charlotte's eyes glanced beyond her tray to where Mezzo and Oliver were sitting on the floor. The two cats were perfectly still, staring straight at Charlotte and Ruth. The empty expressions on the cats' faces caused Charlotte to briefly wonder what they were thinking.

"Do you miss it?" Ruth asked, placing the ball on her lap before wrapping her hands around it as if she were holding a small child.

"Miss what?" Charlotte asked.

"Going to their football games," Ruth stated, her eyes turning to the football on her lap. "It's been years since we've been to a game. Old age has just taken the wind out of my sails for going. Do you miss it? Do you still want to go?"

Charlotte paused for a moment, slipped another chip in her mouth and pondered the right words to use in reply.

"For me, it depends on the time of the year," Charlotte stated before taking a sip of some iced tea. "Now if we're talking about early fall, under a clear blue sky, when the sun is just right...I can feel my heart long for us to be there for the sights and sounds of a football game. However, when it's December or January and it's cold and snowing...I'm quite content sitting on the couch with you."

"I feel exactly the same way," Ruth nodded.

"Do you remember the first time father took us to a Redskins' football game?" Charlotte asked. "I know I'll never forget it because it was also the first time I ever heard him yell."

"He certainly did," Ruth sighed. "He never acted like that around the house."

"Mother wouldn't have allowed it," Charlotte nodded.

"I believe I even heard father curse at one game," Ruth giggled.

"Yes!" Charlotte laughed, pointing to Ruth. "Now that you mention it, he did use some choice words at those games, didn't he?"

"Mother wouldn't have permitted that tone or that language in the house," Ruth stated.

"You're right about that," Charlotte grinned. "She kept us all in line, even father."

"There is one thing I do miss about going to those football games," Ruth grinned, and she sat up a little straighter like she was back in school answering a question. "I miss being able to yell as loud as I want. I always felt better after yelling with father at a Redskins' game. Come to think of it, I don't think I've yelled about anything in years. I've raised my voice every so often, but not to a full-on scream like I would at one of those football games. Even if I tried now, I'm afraid my voice just isn't as strong as it used to be."

"Go ahead and yell during today's game if you want," Charlotte shrugged before gesturing to the floor where Oliver and Mezzo were sitting. "Just know that those two might not like it."

Ruth looked down and grinned at both cats.

"I'll keep that in mind today," she answered.

Charlotte grabbed the TV remote, went to press the power button and then paused when she heard the doorbell ring. She froze, with the remote still pointing at the TV and her finger poised on the *power* button. She turned to Ruth and slowly lowered the remote.

"Please don't answer it," Ruth begged, pointing at the television. "Just turn on the TV and let's both ignore that doorbell."

"But the game doesn't start for ten minutes," Charlotte countered, glancing at her watch.

"I want to hear everything the announcers have to say before the game starts," Ruth explained. "I want all the details. Besides, if we don't answer the door…whoever it is…they'll go away. Now please turn it on."

The doorbell rang again, causing Charlotte to put the remote down on the couch.

"Please, sister!" Ruth begged.

"It might be important, Ruth," she quietly stated.

Charlotte stood up, glanced at a mirror to check her auburn hair, her lipstick, and the wrinkles around her eyes that only seemed more pronounced with her senior years. Having deemed her appearance acceptable, she stepped towards the hallway.

"Wait!" Ruth said in a sharper voice. "If you walk into the hall then they'll know we're here. I'm begging you, sister, please don't go over to the door."

"It is not proper to leave a guest waiting on the front stoop," Charlotte pointed out before entering the hallway.

"Charlotte! Charlotte! Come back here!" Ruth snapped.

"Calm down," Charlotte calmly replied from the hall, "I'm just going to take a peek through a side window."

"Fine!" Ruth grumbled. "But whoever it is…just don't let them see you!"

With Charlotte out of the room, Ruth picked up the TV remote and pressed the power button. Blue sky and an emerald field filled the screen. The sounds of a cheering crowd tickled her ears and she could feel her heart begin to race.

"I've been looking forward to this all week," Ruth enthusiastically explained to both cats.

Mezzo and Oliver, who were seated on the floor in front of her, simply stared back at Ruth while remaining perfectly still.

With the announcers talking about the importance of the game, Ruth noticed something move out of the corner of her eye. She turned to find her sister standing in the hall adjacent to the room. Ruth eagerly pointed to the screen and smiled. Charlotte quietly made her way into the room, grabbed the remote from Ruth's hand, and quickly turned off the TV.

"Hey!" Ruth objected. "Why did you do that?"

"I'm sorry, sister, but we have some company," Charlotte softly explained, putting the remote down on a side table.

Charlotte turned and gestured for a young man to enter the room. At first, Ruth thought it was a high school student selling something. He had blond hair that hung just above his shoulders. He wore faded blue jeans, white sneakers, and a white dress shirt that was untucked. In addition to his short lean frame, the guest's face was quite youthful. In fact, Charlotte couldn't spot one whisker on his face...only a few pimples on either cheek.

As was good manners for any guest, Charlotte forced a smile. Ruth stood up from the couch and did the same. They both recognized the young man standing before them. It was a youthful face, but not the kind that belonged in a high school classroom. Instead, it was a face well-known to most in Washington social circles.

The guest slowly stepped across the room before stopping a few feet away from Ruth.

Charlotte moved beside her sister and focused on the guest. Upon closer inspection, the features on his face simply reinforced what she already knew. He was quite young. Charlotte folded her hands in front of her waist and in a calm tone of voice let one question slip from her lips.

"I'd suppose you're here about the murder...aren't you?"

Chapter 3: The Guest

Ian Walsh is a well-kept secret in Washington's high society. To those who know him, he is a young chef with remarkable talent. A hometown boy, Ian was trained in some of the best restaurants by the finest chefs in the D.C. area. Most agree that Ian is well on his way to becoming a prominent name in the food industry. Yet, what makes him special isn't just his God-given talent for combining spices and flavors. It's how he achieved all of this by the tender age of nineteen. Only the wealthiest in Washington social circles can afford to hire Ian to cater their parties. As many in the know like to say, it's only a matter of time before Ian owns his own restaurant and will no longer make house calls.

"Miss Dupree," Ian finally spoke, lacking the kind of baritone voice that would indicate a change from boyhood to man. His dark eyes flicked between Ruth and Charlotte, realizing that his first two words had already created some unintended confusion. "I mean…both…Miss Duprees. It is so kind of you to see me today. Am I interrupting anything?"

Ruth glared at the darkened TV screen and the spread of snacks on the trays. She lifted the football off her lap and slowly placed it on the cushion beside her.

"Of course not," she quietly fibbed, her eyes lingering on the TV remote on the side table. "It's always a pleasant surprise when a guest stops by to visit on a Sunday afternoon. Even on a chilly one like today."

"Yes," Charlotte smiled to her guest before gesturing towards the room. "You must be freezing, Ian. Please come in and warm up. I can make you some hot tea."

Slipping his hands in his jeans' pockets, he entered the room and settled into a cream-colored chair that practically enveloped his narrow frame. He rubbed his hands together and smiled at his hostesses.

"Tea won't be necessary," he said, nervously running one hand through his hair. "Did you enjoy your dinners at the National Portrait Gala the other night?"

"We did," Ruth quietly answered.

"What you did at the black-tie gala was simply...amazing," Charlotte stated with a broad smile to punctuate her sentiment.

"Yes," Ruth joined in, "the food practically melted in my mouth."

"I heard comments from many guests that reflect my sister's sentiments," Charlotte nodded.

"I heard words like...amazing and sumptuous," Ruth grinned.

"It was so good of you to lend your time to the National Portrait Gallery's Gala,"

Charlotte chimed in. "The museum always gets our support for fundraising. Our parents felt the same way and were generous contributors. That's why we continue to participate in the National Portrait Gallery's Gala. I must say that in all my years of attending...your food has to be at the top of the list for their galas."

When both sisters finished speaking it occurred to them that their guest had yet to utter a single word in reply to their praise. Instead, he remained silent, nervously drumming his fingers on one knee while staring at them.

"Thank you," Ian finally said, his blue eyes dipping down to the floor. "You know, it's nice to hear such complimentary things about my cooking. It seems that the local newspaper pulled their review of my entrees for the National Portrait Gala. At first, I thought the critic had deemed my food unworthy to write about. When I contacted the editor to inquire, I was told there were other factors involved in the decision to drop the review. I'd suppose you two ladies know more about it."

His eyebrows pushed together to form an expression that appeared to be a mix of frustration with a hint of anger.

"We're sorry to hear about your review being scrapped," Charlotte replied, glancing at her sister. "As you are well aware…a terrible situation occurred that night and the police had to be called."

"That's where things get a little fuzzy for me," Ian said, his voice arcing to a higher pitch.

"You see, one minute I'm slaving away over my staff and my stoves and then the police come barging into my kitchen. Of course, when I read the paper the next morning I got a better understanding of what had happened. And, as I said before, I was saddened to find that the quality of my food was not considered newsworthy. However, in the days and weeks that followed I found the newspaper's coverage to be a bit vague on details about what really happened. To be honest, I still don't know what took place. When I complained to the editor about their wayward review of my food he suggested I contact you two for more information about the circumstance at the Gala that night."

Ruth and Charlotte exchanged glances.

"Us?" Ruth asked, looking a bit perplexed.

"I knew the editor's mother," Charlotte calmly replied. "It's nice of him to think so highly of us. Well, what happened that night was, first and foremost, a tragedy. It led to a very convoluted investigation. Of course, the police worked hard to keep the details of the case away from the press. So I can appreciate your frustration, Ian. Especially after reading the articles which, in my opinion, barely scratched the surface as to what really occurred."

"Then tell me more," Ian said, moving to a cream-colored couch where Charlotte was seated. "I'm not the press, Miss Dupree, and I don't gossip. So please tell me what you know. Tell me what bumped my glorious meal from being a featured story."

"Sister," Ruth whispered, her eyes turning to the dark TV screen.

"Very well," Charlotte softly stated, her eyes glancing at Ruth. "I think we can make some time for a story."

Ruth rolled her eyes after hearing those words.

In one swift motion, Charlotte sat back, crossed one leg, and turned her eyes to her guest's face. She closed her eyes for a moment to arrange her thoughts and then she was ready to begin.

Chapter 4: The Tale of Harlan Ellis

If you mention the name "Harlan Ellis" to anyone in D.C. social circles, you'll get mostly smiles and maybe a few kind words in reply. You see, Harlan Ellis is known as the perfect guest to invite to any social event. His value as a guest comes not in his listening skills, but in the many stories he likes to tell and how much those tales can entertain a party.

A man of Washington sensibility and southern charm, Harlan has lived a full rich political life. He freely shares his experiences when attending cocktail parties, luncheons, and political fundraisers. Whether recalling his service in the White House, his time as a Supreme Court clerk, or his personal relationship with two former presidents, Harlan's stories never fail to draw the attention of those people who seek him out for entertainment.

Now at first glance, Harlan does not appear to be the most commanding speaker. He is a short white haired man with a trim build and a delicate voice. His face resembles that of a small boy caught with his hand in the cookie jar. His mouth hangs open quite naturally and his brown eyes look rather sad. Yet, despite his diminutive stature, he has the ability to capture a room with his carefully chosen words. I find his real knack for keeping an audience's attention comes in the form he displays in telling his stories.

There is a slow deliberate rhythm to how he reveals each detail about a person or event. Intimate details that only Harlan could know, or so he likes to say. They are the very kind of details that tend to keep an audience hanging on every word.

Unlike some members of Washington society, Harlan Ellis has never come under much scrutiny. His life-long status as a bachelor has never been questioned. Nor has his propensity for bending the facts to enhance a narrative. Because of his talent for storytelling, Harlan has always been embraced by Washington social circles. He has an open invitation to attend most any function and frequents quite a number of them. He is well liked by almost everyone in Washington. Almost everyone.

The fact that Harlan is an acquired taste occurred to me while I stood in the National Portrait Gallery surrounded by the festivities that made up their annual black-tie gala. The moment we arrived, Ruth ducked into the restroom leaving me to walk around the tables, glancing at names and seating arrangements for dinner. My feet stopped by one table and my eyes zeroed in on my sister's name tag. I quickly realized that instead of sitting with me, Ruth was assigned to another table. Curious, I scanned the other names assigned to sit with her. When I saw Harlan's name card fixed at a spot right next to my sister's seat, I took a deep breath and tried to remain calm.

"Oh dear," were the only words that slipped out.

As I mentioned earlier, Harlan Ellis tends to bend the facts to make a story more interesting. Because Ruth and I were born and raised in Washington, D.C. social circles, we are quite familiar with details on everyone and everything in this town. For many years, our mother was at the center of Washington's social web. With such an upbringing, we know a great deal about the nature of the people in this town. We also tend to be more skeptical of those who claim to know the "truth" behind powerful people...which is why my sister is not very fond of Harlan and his storytelling.

When sitting at social events, listening to him speak, I simply tend to regard Harlan as sideshow entertainment. I take his stories to be innocent fodder meant to be consumed for light entertainment and nothing more. When we come across Harlan at parties, my sister and I exchange glances rather than words. We tend to hold our tongues while Harlan goes on about the latest gossip he's heard...or manufactured. Now, of course, I could have simply reached down and swapped his card with another guest, but the spirit of my mother kept me from doing it.

"It is not a guest's place to attend a party and address the mistakes," my mother would say. "It is a guest's job to respect their host by focusing on what goes right...not wrong."

This rule was at the forefront of my mind when I saw my sister's name sitting beside Harlan Ellis's name. Was it my position to point out the mistake? Was it my responsibility to explain to the host that Harlan and my sister get along like a lighter to gasoline? Or was it Ruth's job to accept the challenge in a manner that would make our mother proud?

"Oh, Charlotte," I heard a voice mumble.

I turned to see Ruth standing next to me, her arms folded, the corners of her lips turned slightly down. Her eyes locked on the table and her head slowly shaking from side to side.

"Do you see that?" Ruth asked, and I could see her eyes squint together the way they do when her blood starts to simmer.

"I just spotted it myself," I quietly nodded.

"Does someone *really* expect me to enjoy my dinner while sitting next to...that...that lapdog?" Ruth asked.

"Oh, sister," I smiled, pointing at her and trying to make light of the situation. "It'll be fine, Ruth. He's harmless. Now please keep your voice down before someone hears you."

"I'm sitting next to a lapdog!" Ruth continued, her voice growing sharper. "How do you expect me to react?"

"He's not a lapdog," I said, my eyes glancing around for any nearby guests who might be listening to my sister's outburst.

"He's small and he barks a lot for attention," Ruth pointed out. "In my book...that's a lapdog."

"He's not a lapdog," I said again.

"He's short and has white hair...like a Maltese," Ruth countered. "I bet if you took down his trousers a tail would pop out!"

I took my hand, gently placed it under Ruth's chin and turned her face to mine.

"Remember what mother would tell us," I advised. "Tonight, we are here to be good guests and not to point out the errors of our hosts. Something else mother would say, "Good guests contribute to a good event...they don't *become* the event." If you keep yelling, *you're* going to become the event, sister."

"Lap dog!" Ruth snapped.

"Hush!" I quickly admonished.

"Lap dog!" she said again.

"Stop!" I demanded and I gestured around the table. "Remember, there will be eight other people sitting with you this evening. Try not to ruin their dinner by debating the merits of every story Harlan shares. Promise me you won't cause a scene."

"If he tells the truth," Ruth pointed out, "I won't have to correct him or make a scene."

"We're not *here* to correct anyone," I said. "We're here to contribute money, and our good nature, to the

National Portrait Gallery this evening. That's what guests do. Promise me you'll behave."

Ruth rolled her eyes at me the way she did as a teenage girl. She grabbed a glass of champagne from a passing waiter, forced a smile and offered one firm nod. Once that agreement was made, we decided to join the other guests in walking around the museum.

Of course, while I use the word "museum," the gallery is more than just a museum. Built in 1962, the National Portrait Gallery was begun to store a growing collection of art that featured famous Americans. Founding fathers, artists, leaders, inventors, and activists are just some of the portraits the gallery has acquired over the years. In time, that collection began to include portraits of American presidents. Whenever we visit the National Portrait Gallery, Ruth and I find ourselves drawn to those presidential portraits. Perhaps it is our way of paying respect to those men who held great power, yet lived under unimaginable pressures. While the museum may hold 23,000 pieces of art inspired by a variety of great Americans, the presidential portraits are the ones that I think hold the most interesting stories.

The collection is kept in a part of the gallery called the Hall of Presidents. Except for the White House, or so I've been told, the Gallery's collection of art depicting American presidents is the largest in the world. Whenever Ruth and I stroll by the portraits, we tend to linger in front of those paintings more than any other collection.

Once in the Hall of Presidents, we study the presidents' faces, look into their eyes and imagine the weight of responsibility they must have carried. We also tend to reminisce when standing in front of portraits of certain presidents we met in person. Some we encountered through our parents as young girls and some we met as adults. Quite often a portrait will spark a memory or recollection about an encounter with one of these historical figures.

"Over there," Ruth gestured, pointing to one corner of the room where a portrait of George W. Bush hung. "I truly do love how he seems to be smiling at his father."

"You say that every time we're in here," I replied, turning to the other side of the room where George Herbert Walker Bush's portrait was displayed. Hung on a wall directly across from George W. Bush, it gave the illusion of father and son grinning at each other from across the room.

"I think it's sweet," Ruth countered.

"Sister," I began, continuing to walk by some other presidential portraits, "I have some trivia for you. Did you know that of all these paintings we look at, there were only two presidents who actually had their portraits redone? I read somewhere that Presidents Lyndon Johnson and Bill Clinton are the only ones to commission a second portrait since they disliked the first ones commissioned by the National Portrait Gallery."

"That's because one was vain and one was just a rascal," Ruth giggled.

"Be that as it may," I said, "an interesting fact to know."

Together we moved down a hall to another collection that focused on the founding of America. Portraits on display for this theme included paintings of famous historical figures like Pocahontas, Alexander Hamilton and Frederick Douglass, to name a few. After moving through this collection, we began to notice signs that we were getting closer to the gala.

Soft orange and yellow accent lighting began to illuminate the walls to the museum. We also began to pass by more groups of gentlemen in black tuxedos and ladies in dark flowing gowns. Ruth and I took in every detail as we followed one hallway leading us out of the gallery and into the Kogod Courtyard, a massive enclosure connected at the very center of the museum. It was where the evening's activities and dinner were about to take place.

Upon entering the courtyard, our eyes were immediately drawn to the thirty-foot high ceilings stretching over us. Dark blue lighting splashed against the exterior walls of the museum that wrapped around us. Ruth and I sat down at one table and began to review the other guests in an attempt to figure out where everyone was going to be seated.

A lovely centerpiece of a dozen red roses was neatly arranged in the middle of the table where we were sitting. With a sweet rose scent filling the air, Ruth and I found it somewhat distracting to keep our focus on the guests circulating around us. However, we both know the importance of taking an inventory of guests when attending any social event. When it comes to parties, every guest brings a resource of topics and knowledge with them. As Ruth and I both know, patience is always the key in picking out which conversation to have with which guest.

Soon music filled the air as guests continued to pour into the courtyard. I heard someone say there was 28,000 square feet of space in the Kogod Courtyard, more than enough to accommodate the gala. Whatever the number, there was plenty of room for us to mingle and circulate with guests.

At events like this, I always find it fascinating to take a moment and watch how disciplined the upper crust of Washington can be when moving around each other. How they exchange smiles that are perfectly pleasant yet not too broad. How their arms sway in controlled calculated motions. How they step with measured slow deliberate strides. They pass by one another with movements so smooth and refined that they barely make a sound. In fact, I swear I could have closed my eyes and not even sensed a large number of people moving around me.

I also began to detect a pattern in the fashion of the people in attendance. How the ladies wore dresses of dark respectable shades to match the November season. Crimson, amber and dark violet were some of the more common tones that caught my attention. I also noticed how the men were resigned to more traditional black and white attire. Whether a tuxedo or a respectable dark suit and matching tie, the gentlemen were required to be classically dressed out of respect for the occasion.

"I always think a man looks handsome in a tux," I observed.

"Yes," Ruth replied, "but we're fortunate to be women, Charlotte. At least we have more colors to choose from in dressing for an event like this."

My eyes were still locked on the guests arriving while I listened to my sister's words.

"You know, Ruth," I said, "I think I enjoy the spring galas better than the ones in winter."

"And why is that?" Ruth asked.

"Because I like brighter colors," I shrugged.

"You do love the spring season more than me," Ruth smiled.

"I think everything is better in the spring," I nodded.

Once everyone was seated, a small jazz band began to play and dinner was served. Ruth and I went to our respective tables where we started the evening with our first course, fresh fruit delightfully arranged in a crystal bowl. Once seated, I acknowledged the faces beside me and began to partake in discussions about the festivities, the guests, the museum and, as is inevitable in

Washington, the political landscape. Names were mentioned. Campaigns were touched on. A few passing comments were offered about a new ballet dancer at the Kennedy Center. All in all, I found the rhythm of the conversations at my table to be quite pleasing. However, in the back of my mind, I kept thinking about my sister and worried about how she was faring sitting next to Harlan.

When the second course was served, I found myself balancing dinner conversation with small bites of Chilled Watercress-Spinach Soup, which was delicious. While my mouth was delighted with each spoonful, my thoughts kept going back to Ruth and my eyes glanced across the room more than once for signs of trouble.

Eventually the third course was served, zucchini fries, which provided just enough flavor that it didn't overwhelm the main course, which was a richly textured steak. While I ate, I noticed familiar sounds of a social gathering reverberating around the courtyard: the soft murmurs of collective conversations, the occasional clanking sounds from utensils gently tapping against fine china, the sharper sounds of dishes being stacked on trays after every course. Soon coffee was offered. Desert was served. Conversations were maintained and the evening commenced at an easy pace. I was well into enjoying my lemon torte when it happened.

The first time I heard that voice yell, I thought someone was arguing with a waiter. As the crowd grew silent, and the yelling continued, I looked up from my steak. I thought that someone was announcing a fire or having a heart attack. While I couldn't see the source of the noise, I quickly discerned it was a man's voice that was yelling. I began to see people at my table turning to the front of the courtyard, so I stopped eating and did the same. When I saw the face of the person doing the shouting I felt my heart jump into my throat. It was Harlan Ellis carrying on about something.

"He sounds upset," I heard a woman next so me say, while taking a bite of her steak.

My thoughts quickly turned to Ruth and I put my fork down. I stood up and caught a glimpse of her sitting at her table, looking quite calm while eating her meal. Her face held no expression. My eyes then turned back to Harlan, who continued to rant and wave his arms in the air. He appeared to be quite upset about something. One possible explanation popped into my head.

"What did you say to upset him, sister?" I whispered to myself.

I sat back down and began to take a deep breath to stay calm. I know my sister. She has a knack for treating people like teapots, raising their temperature just to see them steam. Leave Ruth alone with someone she doesn't care for and she's bound to bring them from a simmer to a boil with a few well-chosen words.

With Harlan continuing to yell and shout, my natural instinct was to blame my little sister for the disturbance. However, when looking at the faces of the people around me reacting to what he was saying, I soon began to realize that this was more than just a temper tantrum. In fact, what Harlan was saying had transformed the festive nature of the courtyard into an air of concern.

I stepped away from my table and moved closer to the front of the room to hear him better. I watched as he paced back and forth, continuing to speak and wave his hands like a fiery minister delivering a sermon. Because the courtyard was so big, the reverberations weren't the best. I kept moving closer until I could finally hear his words.

After a few seconds of listening to Harlan Ellis speak, I could feel my knees buckle. I placed one hand on an empty chair beside me to balance myself. I listened carefully for a few moments more to be certain of the severity of his words. Soon I realized what was driving him to carry on so much. Someone was dead. Someone had been murdered.

Chapter 5: An Inconvenience

As I said before, I've lived in Washington D.C. all my life. My sister and I were raised in Washington's social circles and listened to gossip the way some children listen to nursery rhymes. We've attended society events for more years that we care to admit. Yet, with all of that in mind, I doubt either one of us could ever recall a time when we attended a social engagement that culminated with the police sealing off the exits and questioning the guests.

It was an odd experience to be sequestered for the evening. While the band serenaded us with soft jazz music, and drinks were served, there was a detectable level of tension in the air. However, as I told my sister, if we were to ever be detained by the police for a period of time, the Kogod Courtyard was a lovely place to be stuck. With its climate controlled setting and wonderfully large dimensions, neither my sister nor I ever felt distressed by the circumstance. In fact, we took the time to stroll around the courtyard to marvel at the green trees, pink orchids, and full shrubs that were oblivious to the time of the year.

"Stepping in here is always like…taking a deep breath of spring," I sighed.

"Yes," Ruth nodded. "This courtyard is lovely to come to in the winter."

"Agreed," I nodded, sidestepping one police officer.

Together we strolled up to the front of the courtyard where the band was playing. We paused to watch them perform for a moment, then turned away from the stage to glance back at the crowd. Some guests were seated, tipping back glasses of wine and champagne. Others were on their phones, talking or texting about the experience. A few were standing and speaking with police officers. And standing by the exit, I spotted three officers in a corner with Harlan Ellis, who was continuing to gesture excitedly with his hands while he spoke to them with his high-pitched voice.

"Look at him," I said, pointing in Harlan's direction. "A dead body, police officers everywhere, and Harlan can still stop a group of detectives in their tracks with his animated mannerisms and dramatic way of talking."

We stood silent for a moment, observing Harlan. Then my sister turned to me.

"I wonder why no one is speaking to us?" she asked.

"Do you think we look suspicious?" I laughed.

"No," Ruth replied and she gestured with one hand at the crowd in front of us. "But take a look around, sister. They're speaking to men and women, young and old, all ethnicities. They're pretty much speaking to all kinds of people younger than us. What does that tell you?"

I drew in my breath and took a good long look at the police officers mixing with the beautiful people in the room.

"I don't think they know who the killer is," I observed.

"Exactly what I was thinking," Ruth nodded.

Together we quietly walked away from the band and found a quieter corner of the courtyard to stand. A thought popped into my head and I quickly turned and looked at my sister.

"Do you suppose we should even ask about the victim?" I asked. "I mean, I do feel a bit silly standing here without even knowing who died tonight. I would feel remiss if it was someone we knew because all we're doing is sipping champagne and making small talk about winter fashions."

"I think we owe it to the victim to learn more," Ruth nodded.

I took a deep breath and began to study the room and the people occupying it. There were so many faces to consider for information. Together we started to walk around the room, circling the crowd the way a bird might circle potential nourishment. Nourishment, for us, being facts.

Now, for the average person, attending a party with a group this size would simply mean spending time with a random group of people. However, to a person with knowledge of Washington society, this was more than just walking around and looking at the faces of strangers. What I was doing was studying a landscape of social resources.

While we walked, I could see how each face represented a potential source for information. There were some guests who I knew were quite knowledgeable about the people in this town, some guests who I knew were oblivious to D.C. society and a few who were simply unreliable. Ruth and I needed someone who was high up in Washington's social status. Someone who would be a good source for some insight into what was happening. After considering many guests, I finally found the social resource I was looking for. The one person who I knew could shed some light on the evening's events.

"That's who we need to talk to," I said, my eyes locking on my target.

Standing in a sea of sharply dressed young men and elegant young women, Constance Sweeny was easy to spot. A short woman with closely cropped ashen hair and glasses, she wore a dark dress that concealed her generous proportions. She was easy to spot, standing by herself while sipping on a glass of something. When I drew closer, I quickly spotted the birth mark on Constance's right cheek, which I always thought resembled a stray shard of thin red seaweed.

"Hello, Charlotte," Constance said the moment we stepped in front of her. Her eyes turned to my sister and forced one quick smile in Ruth's direction.

"Quite a night," I commented.

"It certainly is," Constance replied, taking one last sip from her glass. Without hesitation, she turned, placed the empty glass on the tray of a passing waiter and quickly removed a full glass from the same tray. "My husband told me they haven't had this many police officers in here since 1984. Back then, the crime was a theft of some Civil War letters. Nothing on the scale of what is happening this evening."

"I would imagine your husband has been quite busy tonight," Ruth observed while we watched Constance sip more champagne.

"You poor dear," I added.

"Unfortunately I haven't seen him since all this happened," she frowned, nervously tugging at a string of pearls that hung from her neck. "It wasn't supposed to be like this, ladies. It was his night off. We were supposed to relax, enjoy a lovely dinner and mingle with our friends. Maybe even dance. I'd suppose when you're in charge of security at this museum…the job never stops."

"Do you know what happened?" Ruth asked.

Constance took me by my elbow and gently pulled me towards her. Ruth also took one step closer to me, her eyes wide with anticipation.

"A body was found," Constance spoke just above a whisper. "Someone found a body in the Men's Room."

"A body?" I asked. "You mean…a…"

"Yes," Constance quietly stated. "A dead body on the floor in the one stall. Trousers down to his knees, I'm afraid. He was lying by the toilet, or so I heard one officer tell my husband. Quite a way to go...if you ask me."

"Oh dear," I replied.

"That's why my husband has been so busy," Constance sighed, shaking her head and turning her eyes to the middle of the courtyard.

"Aren't there security cameras that could help him?" Ruth asked.

"Unfortunately, there are no cameras installed in or around the bathrooms," Constance replied.

After that statement, Constance took a slow deep sip of white wine from her glass.

"So there may be a murderer in this room?" I asked.

Constance merely nodded her head.

Glancing around at the many familiar faces I saw in attendance, it was hard for me to believe that one of these well-dressed ladies or gentlemen had taken a life tonight. Especially since I knew many of the faces quite well.

"Oh my," Ruth said, her hand covering her mouth.

"Do you know who was murdered, Constance?' I asked.

She looked left and right, stepped about two inches from my face and whispered, "Webb Mills."

Chapter 6: Webb Mills

My sister and I had known Webb Mills for many years. He was a tall proud southern gentleman with a naturally red face. He wore his God-given sunburn year-round. When he grew angry, or added some passion to what he was saying, Webb's face actually transformed from a bright red to a darker shade of maroon. His voice also dropped to an octave that was so low it was equivalent to a basso profundo, which is the lowest voice anyone will ever hear singing at an opera. Webb was a tall burly man with big hands and a robust laugh. In addition to politics, he was also passionate about the South and proud of the influence it had on him. His wife, Daisy Mills, was also a product of a southern upbringing. Together they brought a welcome charm to a city that was too caught up in the trappings of power.

Webb had been a political operative for many years. He managed campaigns and built a national consulting business staffed with the best minds in politics. His wife would be the first to tell you that he lived for the next election, regardless of whether it was presidential or congressional. He even owned a private jet that was ready to take him anywhere in a moment's notice. Webb used the jet frequently during election season. With more than two decades of campaign slogans, brilliant strategies, and influential ads to his credit, Webb was well thought of by most in Washington. Before I could get some more details from Constance, she was chasing after another waiter with her empty glass.

"Poor Daisy," Ruth sighed, rubbing her arms like a chill just struck her. "I just saw her a few weeks ago at a luncheon. She was so happy. She told me that she and Webb had just become grandparents for the seventh time. She said how much they were looking forward to going back home to meet their new grandson. I can't believe he's...dead."

The thought of Webb being murdered simply made me numb. I checked my watch, sat down and rested my elbows on the table before folding my hands together.

"What are you doing?" Ruth asked.

"We've done our due diligence," I sighed, my eyes turning down to the table cloth. "Webb Mills died tonight. I don't feel like talking anymore. For now, I think I just want to sit here and think about him. Reflect on some memories. Is that okay with you, sister?"

Ruth nodded and dropped in the seat beside me. Together we watched police officers disperse around the courtyard, taking pictures, writing notes, and speaking with guests. Ruth drew her elbows up on the table. I slumped back into my chair. Together we sat, both displaying the kind of posture that our mother would scold us for. However, as the hours went by, it was clear that proper posture and etiquette were no longer important. On this night, reflection superseded good manners.

My mind began to fill with memories of Webb Mills. I recalled when we first met, and how our relationship began as social acquaintances many years ago. After seeing Daisy and Webb for a few years, it became apparent to the four of us that we weren't going to be leaving Washington any time soon. Both the Mills and us owned homes in Washington. Both of us were long-time residents of the city. Over time Ruth even struck up a good friendship with his wife, Daisy. They discovered a mutual love of art. Whenever there was a new exhibit in town, Daisy was the first person Ruth would call. In addition to discussing the latest art collections in the city, Daisy and Ruth began to find other topics of conversation to enjoy. Travel, movies and family were just some subjects they began to touch on more frequently.

While Ruth and Daisy grew closer over the years, Webb was a different story. He was a political consultant and worked all the time running campaigns and counseling candidates. On the occasions I observed him at parties, I found Webb to be even tempered, well-informed on all topics of conversation, and soft spoken when he had a thought or perspective to share. As the years went by, Webb's sentiments became more valued by those in Washington's social circles. On the occasions that the majority of guests at a party would discuss a candidate, politician, or piece of legislation, it was usually Webb who would be asked for the final say on the matter. Whenever he spoke, everyone in the room grew quiet and listened to every word.

I also learned, though Ruth's conversations with Daisy, that Webb wasn't just focused on his candidates and how to help them win. He was also a man with a good heart. When his church needed a new roof, Webb paid for the work on the condition of anonymity. When a staff member's father suddenly passed away, it was Webb who paid for the cost of the funeral. Through our conversations with Daisy, Webb became more than just a face we recognized. He became a fully formed person. All of this came back to me in a matter of minutes. A rush of images filled my head while the band played, the police questioned guests, and we remained in the National Portrait Gallery well into the night.

Chapter 7: Signs of the Season

In November, the cold air typically moves in from the north with large rude gusts before settling in for the season. This year we were lucky to avoid those cold November winds. After a brief cold snap, the southern winds resurrected and the pleasant autumn temperatures returned. This new weather pattern contributed to the illusion that balmy weather might just usher in the New Year. However, despite the warmer than usual temperatures, there were still signs around D.C. that winter was close at hand.

The National Christmas Tree could be seen on the grounds of the White House. The Capitol Christmas Tree was also on display at Capitol Hill. The Washington Ballet began to advertise their production of The Nutcracker. Even the radio was playing more Christmas songs. All were pleasant indications of the upcoming holiday season. While I find all of these signs very pleasing, there is one smaller sign I tend to focus on to indicate to me that the winter season has arrived. To find this detail, my sister and I have only to travel to the National Gallery of Art's Sculpture Garden.

During the spring and summer months, the Sculpture Garden is a busy place. It provides a lovely combination of walking paths, flowers and contemporary sculptures for tourists to enjoy. At the center of the garden is a wonderfully large fountain where visitors are welcome to sit, slide their toes into the water and cool off. Since the proportions of the oval shaped fountain are so big, the museum is able to transform the structure into an ice rink for the winter. The rink is open to the public during November and December. So on a crisp December morning, under blue skies and sunshine, I decided to venture out with my sister to see the ice rink for the first time this season.

Once we arrived, we picked up some hot chocolate from a nearby café. While some onlookers preferred to stand by the rink, Ruth and I sat on a nearby bench, enjoyed the sunshine and watched the activity on the ice.

From our vantage point, we could see both young and old skaters circling around the ice. A few parents stood at the side of the rink and called out to their children when they passed. Young couples held hands while skating. A few tourists took pictures. All in all, it was a lovely scene and it reminded me of winters past when, as young girls, father would take us skating.

"That used to be us," I said to Ruth, gesturing to two little girls skating by with what I guessed was a young father between them holding their hands

"Yes," Ruth smiled. "I can still see us, walking with father down to the National Mall, slipping on our skates, and joining him for an afternoon of gliding up and down the frozen Reflecting Pool."

"I quite enjoyed that," I nodded. "Skating on the Reflecting Pool with the Lincoln Memorial on one side of me and the Washington Monument on the other. They were such special days."

Both of us paused, blew into our hot chocolate and took a sip.

"With all due respect to the Sculpture Garden," Ruth observed, "the atmosphere at the Reflecting Pool was much nicer."

"This rink is very nice," I nodded, "but there's barely enough room for everyone. We had so much more room to skate on the Reflecting Pool."

"You used to be able to do jumps," Ruth recalled.

"I did," I nodded, "back when my knees were much younger."

"Looking at these poor people," Ruth said, waving her hand towards the rink. "They're bunched so close together no one would dare try a jump or a pirouette for fear of knocking other people down. It's a shame they stopped that tradition of opening the Reflecting Pool for public skating."

"I agree," I nodded before taking a sip of her hot chocolate. "Someone told me they closed it for safety concerns but...if someone fell through the ice the water wasn't *that* deep. To the best of my recollection, nothing in the Reflecting Pool was ever damaged and no one was hurt."

Ruth remained silent for a moment. She smiled and nodded at the festive scene.

"I must say, Charlotte," she began, "it is nice to be in the company of people who are laughing and smiling and not just indulging in gossip."

The comment caught me off guard. I turned and looked at her.

"Why, Ruth," I grinned, "that's quite a surprising thing to hear from you. After a party, you're usually the first one to share what rumors you overheard when we get home."

"Well, maybe Harlan Ellis has changed my mind about doing that," Ruth mumbled in a way that sounded like she was almost embarrassed to admit.

"Harlan?" I joked. "Perhaps I should write him a little note to thank him for curing you of that terrible habit."

Ruth's face turned bright red. I knew the comment would lead to a sharp rebuke from my sister. I swear I could even see her backbone straighten and her head quickly snapped in my direction.

"You like gossip just as much as I do!" Ruth loudly pointed out.

"You're right," I laughed, "but I'm not the one who said Harlan *cured* me of enjoying good gossip."

"Fair enough," she nodded before taking another sip of hot chocolate. "Well, maybe it's not the rumor spreading that bothers me. Maybe it's the lies he tells in the form of a rumor. I think that's at the heart of how I'm feeling right now."

"And how do you know which of his statements *are* lies?" I asked.

"Everything he says is a lie," Ruth explained. "Nobody seems to notice that but us."

"Then perhaps we should make his fabrications a bit more...obvious...to everyone," I suggested, before finally taking my first sip of hot chocolate.

"What do you mean?" Ruth asked.

"Might I suggest we spy on him," I replied.

Ruth slowly shook her head.

"I'm not sitting outside of his apartment peeking through the windows at him in his pajamas," Ruth complained.

"That's not I what I'm suggesting," I quickly clarified. "My plan is we follow him to some parties, listen to his conversations and point out the inconsistencies in what he says to the other guests. We use his words against him, sister. That's how mother always caught us telling a fib when we were girls. I swear she kept a transcript in her head of everything we said and when the time was right...she used our words against us."

"I like that idea," Ruth said. She turned to me with a grin on her lips. "Now as we both know, Charlotte, one of us is good at speaking in front of groups of people and one of us is better at being a quality listener. I just want to be clear about our...talents so we know which one of us will be listening... I mean spying on Harlan."

I simply smiled at my sister's logic, knowing that her logic had just sealed my fate.

Chapter 8: The Party Boy

For the rest of the week, Ruth and I maintained a busy schedule, attending a wide range of social events. A reception for a newly appointed diplomat from England. A fundraiser for a Representative from the House who was laying a foundation for her run for the Senate. Also, a luncheon for a former First Lady who was reaching out to her elite supporters to raise funds for her husband's Presidential Library. All in all, a busy stretch.

Also attending each of these events was Harlan Ellis. Like us, Harlan frequented social gatherings on a regular basis. Thus, it was quite easy to shadow his schedule. The fact that he had witnessed a murder the previous week seemed to propel him even deeper into the social circles of Washington.

Whenever we found Harlan at a social engagement, he was usually surrounded by onlookers as he recounted his tale of the murder at the National Portrait Gallery. While my sister did not have the stomach to listen to him speak, I was curious about the death and wanted to learn more details. After all, Webb Mills was a friend. I owed it to him to learn more about the circumstances around his death.

At each event we attended, I made a point of lingering in the same room as Harlan to listen to his account of Webb's death. Of course, Harlan couldn't begin by talking about what a good man Webb Mills was. How he was a good husband and loving grandfather. That kind of news was too common to keep people around him. Instead, Harlan always chose to slip right into the gutter with how he presented his recollection.

He'd usually begin by speaking of a woman he suspected Webb was having an affair with. He'd also mention two Representatives with political axes to grind with Webb for some dirty tricks he pulled in campaigns. Were they angry enough to commit murder? Harlan would suggest as much but leave the question unanswered. Then, of course, there was the widow, scorned more than once by her husband's infidelities...or so Harlan claimed. Perhaps she was capable of killing him, or so Harlan implied for his audience to consider. This last statement caused a few gasps to be heard from his audience, which led to the slightest of smiles to appear on Harlan lips. The grin, in my opinion, resembled that of a mischievous garden gnome.

As for the crime itself, I was disappointed that Harlan would offer few details of what he witnessed. At one party, he recalled that the restroom had poor lighting, and the murderer was "on top of me before I knew it." At another gathering, I can recall Harlan stating how he was knocked to the floor "as that deranged killer" ran off. At every social event he attended, Harlan stated he did not get a good look at the murderer's face, but he was more than willing to list a few possible suspects. It was like he could sense that his audiences didn't crave facts, just names and wild innuendos.

In addition to his dramatic presentations, I began to notice a pattern with Harlan's performances. At every event, there was a shifting narrative to Harlan's recollections. A change in facts that I began to detect. After listening to his account multiple times, I noticed how Harlan would change the details, vary descriptions, even insert names of suspects that I was quite certain weren't even in attendance that night. Part of me knew it was his attempt to entertain. It also made me curious to know what he *really* saw.

In the end, I just wanted to know which facts were accurate and which were fabricated. I knew I'd have to listen very carefully to differentiate between the two. I also knew I'd have to attend more functions with Harlan to separate fact from fiction.

Chapter 9: Crumpets and a Scandal

The best way to wake the body is to rouse the mind.

My father would share that bit of wisdom with me and my sister every morning while he read the newspaper over breakfast. As young girls, Ruth and I would quietly sit at the breakfast table struggling to wake up between sips of juice and bites of toast. Father, on the other hand, was more outgoing. He'd drink coffee and chat with mother at great length about the events featured in the newspaper.

I can still picture him sitting at the kitchen table. His head tilted to one side while he studied each page. His glasses always halfway down the slope of his nose. His fingers stroking his thick dark hair while he read. His voice calling across the table to our mother about what he felt were crucial facts about an article. However, there was only one thing at the breakfast table that would always cause father to put down the newspaper.

It was on those mornings when our maid would prepare homemade crumpets for breakfast. She'd lather them in butter with a thin layer of strawberry jam. On those mornings, father would put the paper aside, fill the air with compliments to our maid and savor every bite. When he'd leave for work after having crumpets for breakfast, father would always step out the door with a smile on his face.

Sixty years later, Ruth and I still maintain our father's philosophy of starting each day by rousing the mind as well as enjoying our breakfast. While neither one of us ever learned how to make crumpets, we do maintain the most important morning tradition of a Dupree household. We start the day by filling our minds with ideas while filling our stomachs with food.

Like we did years ago, Ruth and I still start each morning seated at the same kitchen table we ate at as girls. Like father, we read each section of the newspaper and discuss the events of the day. Some mornings, I even notice the way Ruth resembles father in how her head tilts to one side while she reads. I'm also aware of how my reading glasses, like father's, tend to slide halfway down the slope of my nose when I study the paper. Since we've lived in the same house all of our lives, breakfast is the one time of the day when I feel our father's spirit the most. We even tend to leave his seat at the table vacant out of habit.

"They *finally* printed a brief article about what happened at the gala!" Ruth announced with a mix of relief and frustration in her voice.

"Well it took them long enough," I mumbled while preparing my oatmeal by the stove.

"Listen to this," Ruth replied.

I turned to the kitchen table where Ruth was sitting. The morning paper was still folded and on her lap. Her one elbow was planted firmly on the table. Her head tilted to one side while resting on her hand. Her eyes were staring down at one section of the paper and she didn't blink once.

"Police were summoned to the National Portrait Gallery on Monday night," she read. "While little is known as to the reason why, officials stated that no pieces of art were harmed and no thefts occurred. A gala was being held by the museum but officials stated that no guests were in any danger throughout the evening. An official statement on the events would be released at a later time."

Ruth closed this section of the paper and her eyebrows mashed together as they typically did to reflect her frustration with something.

"Webb Mills deserved more than a vaguely detailed column on page five near the police log," Ruth fumed before taking a sip of coffee. "Why didn't they say he was murdered?"

"You're right," I nodded. "Webb deserved front page status. He ran campaigns and helped to shape the country's political landscape. He also got some questionable candidates elected, in my opinion, but also a lot of good people. Sometimes he showed poor judgment in how he ran his campaigns but we all have our flaws."

"Are you saying they buried the story because he wasn't a saint?" Ruth observed.

"Not necessarily," I sighed, and I turned back to the stove to stir a small pot of oatmeal. "I'm just saying his line of work led him to push hard for his candidates. When you make politics your lifetime profession your hands are going to get dirty doing your job. You know this very well, sister. Perhaps he rubbed some news editors the wrong way in trying to get them to give favorable coverage to his candidates."

"That may be true," Ruth nodded, still staring at the article. "but he was a good husband, sister. Despite what that...that...Lapdog has been saying around town, Webb was always faithful to Daisy."

"When you say...Lapdog...do you mean Harlan?" I asked.

"I've decided from now on I'm going to refer to him as '*Lapdog*'," Ruth smirked.

"Well that's mature," I mumbled.

"I've heard enough of his yapping about Webb having an affair," Ruth continued. "I can tell you that he and Daisy were happily married. In fact, Daisy told me once that she and Webb had an agreement to never dine without the other. Webb went to extraordinary lengths to stay here in Washington, D.C., while overseeing campaigns around the country. He had a devoted staff and his words were like gold to anyone who would conference call him. On those rare occasions when he had to leave the city on his private jet, Daisy told me that Webb would take her with him. Those two were never apart until…the other night."

"Poor Daisy," I sighed, scooping out some oatmeal into a small bowl.

"I can only imagine how she's holding up," Ruth nodded while turning to another section of the paper. With my oatmeal finally at a reasonable temperature, I leaned one hip against the counter and began to dip my spoon into the small bowl I was holding before taking a bite.

"You and Daisy have been good friends for a long time," I began, feeling some agreeably warm oatmeal go down my throat. "We should stop by to offer our condolences to her. I mean…that's the least friends can do, right?"

"A good idea," Ruth nodded.

"I'll pick up a sympathy card at the store and we can swing by to see her," I continued. "She's known us for a long time. Sometimes, when a tragedy like this occurs an old friend can be the best medicine."

Chapter 10: Dinner with Daisy

Much to my surprise, Ruth was actually able to reach Daisy Mills by phone later that morning. After a brief conversation, my sister surprised me yet again by stating she had scheduled a dinner date with the newly widowed Mrs. Mills for later that evening.

Rather than allowing my thoughts to dwell on the meeting, I tried to keep myself busy for the rest of the morning and the afternoon. I began with some household chores, then wrote a few correspondences to friends, then decided to clean out our cat's litter box before the smell became unbearable. When the hour finally arrived to meet Daisy, we took a cab to Martin's Tavern, which is a lovely restaurant at the corner of Wisconsin Avenue in Georgetown.

Built in 1933, Martin's Tavern has seen its share of famous customers come and go over the years. In fact, it's well known to a lot of Washington insiders that every sitting president since Harry Truman has dined at Martin's Tavern at least once. With its hardwood floors, sweeping bar, and soft lighting the Tavern makes for a quaint dining experience. Yet, what makes it unique in D.C. are the plaques marking the booths and tables where famous people have dined. Upon arriving at Martin's Tavern, patrons are given a choice of sitting in some interestingly named booths. The *Madeleine Albright Booth*, the *Harry Truman Booth*, and the *Richard Nixon Booth* are just some of the booths named after famous patrons. For romantics, there is even a spot called the *Proposal Booth*.

As legend has it, John Kennedy first asked Jackie for her hand in marriage while they dined in Martin's Tavern. The booth they ate in is now named the *Proposal Booth*. Ruth and I have eaten at Martin's Tavern many times. Whenever we go for lunch or dinner, my sister always orders the Lobster Risotto while I'm more partial to the Pasta Primavera.

The moment we stepped into Martin's Tavern for our dinner date with Daisy, loud laughter erupted from the bar, filling our ears while we waited to be seated.

"Sounds like quite a crowd having drinks after work," I observed.

"Four people does not constitute a crowd, sister," Ruth replied, peeking over at the bar.

"Just a figure of speech," I sighed, checking my watch.

While we waited, I pondered the years that we'd known Daisy. How Webb, Daisy, Ruth and I began to meet at social events. How we chatted and discovered a mutual love for the ballet. How we began attending performances together at the Kennedy Center. There was one instance I can recall when our relationship with Daisy and Webb became more personal. It was a few winters back, while attending a ballet, when Ruth had a dreadful cold. She had a terrible cough all during the first act. I was concerned it was something more than a cold. The next day, Daisy surprised us by delivering some homemade soup that she swore would cure Ruth of that terrible cough. It was such a sweet gesture and the soup actually did help. While Ruth eventually shook off her cold, she took Daisy's concern to heart. That's when a social acquaintance blossomed into a true friendship between Daisy and Ruth.

My recollections were interrupted by a sudden gust of cold air blowing into the restaurant. I turned to see Daisy Mills stepping inside and quickly closing the door behind her. Wrapped in a full-length black sable coat, she made eye contact with us and paused for a moment to fix her hair and push aside some of her blond-gray locks from her eyes. Daisy was always careful to maintain an elegant appearance, even with a north wind howling through the streets of Georgetown.

"Look at her," Ruth whispered. "I know she's our age but...she looks ten years younger than us, doesn't she?"

"The years have always been kind to Daisy," I whispered back.

Daisy walked up to us and I could tell by the size of her blue eyes that she was cold from the wind blowing her through the front door. She slipped off her coat revealing her narrow frame. She tucked the coat under one arm and stepped closer to us.

"Good to see you two," she offered in a soft voice.

"Hello, Daisy," Ruth said before giving her a hug.

When Ruth finished her embrace, I stepped up and did the same.

"How are you holding up?" I heard Ruth ask in a soft voice.

Daisy looked at both of us, forced a smile and nodded her head. Words were still hard to come by to describe her feelings, or so I thought.

"We're glad you're here," I offered.

A waiter finally greeted us and directed us to a table beneath a quaint chandelier. Crisp white napkins were placed before us in a fan-fold shape. A soft glow emanated from a candle at the center of the table. I could see Daisy's eyes focus on the candle while Ruth and I removed our coats.

"Winter feels like it's coming," Ruth said.

"It does," Daisy nodded and she picked up her napkin and slowly opened it. "I know it's only been a week. I know it's still the same season that it was last week...but for me...the world just *feels* different. It's like...I'm sitting here with you two...and I've known you both for many years...but spending time with you tonight just feels different. Even this restaurant, which Webb and I have come to many times...it just doesn't feel the same to me."

"That's understandable," I nodded. "I'd imagine losing Webb has changed many things for you."

"So how are you coping, Daisy?" Ruth asked.

"Some days I do okay," Daisy nodded. "I try to keep busy. Lately, I've been pretending Webb is just on one of his business trips, running one of his campaigns from another state, bound to be home for dinner, which is what he'd always try to do. Most days we'd always be together for dinner. I know it's silly...but sometimes it helps me to get through the day by thinking he's just off running a campaign somewhere."

"If I may ask," I gently inquired. "Have you made any arrangements yet?"

"Arrangements?" Ruth asked, head tipping slightly to one side.

"You know...a funeral," I clarified, glancing at my sister. "I mean, we've known each other for a long time, Daisy. Ruth and I just want to know when we can attend the funeral to pay our respects."

"There won't be a funeral," Daisy smiled. "I'm taking Webb back to North Carolina for burial. Just family will be there. You see, many years ago Webb picked out two plots in a cemetery that overlooks a valley at the base of the Blue Ridge Mountains. Oh, how Webb loved those mountains. He would always point them out to me whenever that ridge was visible. He loved them. I think that's why he picked that cemetery for us to be buried."

"Didn't you have a say in deciding where your burial spot was going to be?" Ruth asked.

"Webb was always more practical about such matters," Daisy stated, rubbing her hands together over the candle. "I tend to live for the moment. Webb always saw the bigger picture. When we became grandparents for the first time, he felt it was time to find our burial plots. I let him take care of that. I preferred to focus on snuggling with our first grandchild...not talking about cemeteries."

The conversation stalled with the arrival of the waiter, who spoke about the specials, passed out some menus, and took orders for drinks. The moment the waiter stepped away from the table, Ruth leaned forward in her seat and looked at me and Daisy.

"I don't like when a waiter or waitress says they'll be 'taking care of me,'" Ruth commented. "It makes it sound like they'll be wiping my nose and rubbing my toes while I eat. Just take my order and be done with all that silly chitchat."

The observation brought out a very brief smile from Daisy, like a hint of sunshine on an otherwise dull day. I noticed our waiter, who was standing close by, looked none too pleased with my sister's comment.

"As I've done more than once in my life...I apologize for my sister," I smiled to Daisy.

"It's okay," Daisy replied, turning to Ruth. "It's the first time someone almost made me laugh this week."

I reached across the table and gently rested my hand on Daisy's two cold hands. Her bumpy knuckles, ravaged from arthritis, fit snuggly under my hand.

"I can only imagine what it must be like to lose a spouse...but then to have the police involved...it must be terrible," I sighed.

"Have they spoken to you?" Ruth asked.

"A phone call is the least they should do," I nodded. "Have they told you if they sorted anything out about what happened that night? I mean Harlan Ellis was carrying on but I don't trust anything that comes out of that man's mouth."

"They promised to call with news but I haven't heard from them yet," Daisy softly answered, her eyes glancing back to the candle. "They spoke to me once…that was the night of the gala when they told me they found a rope around my dear husband's…neck."

"A rope?" I asked, leaning forward in my seat.

"They think it came from a janitor's closet," Daisy recalled, her eyes locked on the candle flame again. "That's the only detail I know. Just thinking about how he must have suffered…those last few seconds being choked like that…poor Webb. I do hope that he passed out before he…"

She dipped her head forward over the table, folded her hands as if she were about to pray and rested her forehead on them. I felt badly for leading the conversation to this point so early in the evening.

"There, there," Ruth said, reaching over and rubbing Daisy's back. "Perhaps we should spend some time looking at the menu. Change the focus to food and lighter topics."

As the evening wore on, and our meals were served, the conversation flowed with more emotional stability. The topics moved freely from grandchildren, to our cats, to the last election Webb ran for a Representative from Maine, to the latest showings at various art galleries in town. After nearly bringing Daisy to tears at the start of the evening, Ruth and I worked hard to turn the occasion into a more pleasant experience during our entree.

By the time dessert was served, we were all smiling and enjoying a lovely *crème brulée* served with a small scoop of warm caramel. The mood at the table was more pleasant. Listening to Ruth and Daisy chat about a mutual friend running for re-election in the House, I decided it was time to ask one more difficult question about the murder.

"Daisy," I began, leaning across the table. "Listening to you two talk about a campaign made me think of Webb. Was there any campaign he ran that didn't end on good terms? I'm not talking about the campaigns that he lost. I mean were there *any* campaigns that just didn't end well between him and the candidate."

"What my sister means is if you can think of someone angry enough to kill Webb?" Ruth asked in her usual blunt way.

My head snapped at my sister and I could feel my face grow flushed. Ruth's eyes grew wide and her mouth quickly clamped shut but it was too late. The damage was done. We both turned to Daisy, whose face was no longer smiling. In fact, the expression it held was quite rigid and the corners of her mouth were turned down. I glared at my sister the way I used to when we were teenaged girls and she'd lose her temper and say something angry to our mother. Being the older sister meant I always had to have more self-control about what flew out of my mouth. Ruth was the opposite. She was always more impulsive and whatever words she harbored in her head always seemed to find their way out of her lips.

"I was trying to be more tactful, Ruth," I whispered.

"I'm sorry," Ruth whispered back, her eyes turning down to her dessert. "Maybe I'll just scoop a spoonful of dessert in my mouth and keep quiet for the rest of the evening."

"It's okay," Daisy began, raising her hand to both of us. "Really, what Ruth asked was a valid question. I'll tell you both what I told the police at the gala. I can't think of anyone who would want to harm my husband. Webb had a challenging job, but he always left his campaigns and his clients on good terms. That's why they would call him to run re-election campaigns more than once. Webb never left a client on bad terms because he knew one day that client might need him again. He was very aware of how power worked and he was careful not to let himself become corrupted by it. That's why he ran campaigns for both parties...but never stepped over the line and ran himself. So to answer your question, Ruth, I don't know anyone who would hold a grudge against my husband."

After dinner, we left the restaurant and walked Daisy to the curb where a taxi was waiting. We exchanged hugs with her and watched her get in. The second Daisy's taxi sped away, Ruth's hand shot straight up in the air to hail another cab for us. The wind was not as strong, but it was dark and the winter air was noticeably colder than when we arrived. I stood with my arms wrapped across my chest watching Ruth wave wildly at passing traffic.

"Why don't we go inside and have the restaurant call us a taxi," I suggested while stamping my feet on the pavement to stay warm.

"Be patient!" Ruth snapped.

Almost on cue, two headlights swerved towards us and came to a stop. Ruth quickly opened the door to the taxi and hopped in with me close behind her. I was pleasantly surprised at how warm the cab was once I closed the door. As the driver swerved into traffic, I could feel my face and legs begin to thaw. Ruth provided our address to the driver who accelerated down the street, cutting off a car before taking a sharp right turn at an intersection. Ruth and I felt our heads snap back in our seats as the driver accelerated through a light that was about to turn red.

"Did you tell him we're in a hurry...because we aren't!" I commented to Ruth while holding onto the door handle.

"Apparently, *he's* the one in a hurry," Ruth observed as we sped through another traffic light flickering from yellow to red.

"What did you think about Daisy?" Ruth asked. "I think she's holding up very well when you consider everything that's happened."

"Yes," I nodded. "You can tell that Webb kept her in a cocoon."

"How so?" she asked.

"Politics was his career," I continued. "We both know you don't make politics your life's work without making some enemies. Politics by its very nature is combative. At the end of an election, there's a winner and a loser and what separates them can be the result of a few bent facts, some untruths and maybe a dirty trick or two. Many a good person has been slandered when running for office. I just find it hard to believe that Webb ended every campaign on good terms with his clients."

"You know what Mark Twain said about politicians?" Ruth smirked. "I believe he said, 'politicians and diapers must be changed often, and for the same reason.'"

I couldn't help but laugh a little at my sister's quote. She has a long list of quotes in her head ready to use for any occasion.

"Many a good man and woman have gotten their hands dirty in politics," I sighed. "There's no reason for me to believe that Webb faired any differently."

"Which is probably why he had a rope around his neck," Ruth pointed out.

"Perhaps," I nodded. "I think it would be wise of us to talk to someone other than Daisy. It's clear to me that

Webb kept her insulated from his work. We need to find someone who can give us an honest picture of Webb and his dealings over the years."

"I'd be interested in knowing what the police think," Ruth chimed in.

With the city lights flickering by my window at an alarming rate, we took one more hard right turn in our wild cab ride before we stopped in front of our home. Ruth paid the driver while I quickly escaped from the vehicle.

"Hurry up, Ruth!" I called out. "Get out of the cab before that…Mr. Toad takes us for another wild ride!"

As soon as Ruth stumbled out, I slammed the taxi's door shut and it roared off in a cloud of fumes. Ruth and I quietly passed through the wrought iron gate that surrounds our property and stepped into our warm home.

As we took off our coats, I glanced down at the morning paper folded on a side table. There I spotted an article about a police officer who was under investigation for bribery. I looked at the name of the reporter who wrote the article. The mere sight of the name was familiar to me. It gave me an idea for whom we could talk to for some impartial information about Webb and his many clients.

Chapter 11: The Facts

Neil Cabbott is a friend of ours. We met him shortly after he arrived in Washington nearly two years ago. He is gainfully employed as a reporter for one of Washington's largest newspapers. Every so often when we read an article by Neil we comment on the content of his piece and the quality of his writing. A young man from Logan, Iowa, Neil is like a flower that Ruth and I have nurtured since he moved to the city.

When we first met him, Neil had only lived in Washington for a week. He knew very little about the city and the people who lived in it. In two years, we've watched Neil grow from a lost soul to a true Washington insider. As a newspaper reporter, he has developed good sources for his features, which tend to focus on crimes and the police. Ruth and I are proud to consider him our friend. So when we had questions about the police investigation into Webb's death, Neil seemed like a logical choice to contact for more information.

One afternoon we invited Neil over for a visit. When he arrived, he took the time to walk around the house with us and notice a few holiday decorations we had on display. They were small and discreetly displayed, but Neil was quick to notice. After talking about the décor, we surprised Neil by telling him we were taking him out for lunch. Needless to say, Neil was very happy to hear our offer. Without hesitation, he chose Gadsby's Tavern, a lovely old establishment built in the 1700s. There are a lot of restaurants in Washington, but not many can count George Washington, Thomas Jefferson and John Adams as former patrons. Gadsby's Tavern is one of them.

After a few minutes of small talk and catching up, I called for a cab. A few minutes later the three of us were piling into the back of a taxi and heading south along the Potomac River to the restaurant. Much to our relief, this taxi driver appeared to be in no hurry to drop us off, which gave us a few minutes to talk.

"Look at those pieces of ice along the Potomac," Ruth observed. "You can tell winter is finally here."

"That may be true," I grinned, "but it won't cancel our plans for today."

"You really don't have to do this," Neil said.

"It's our treat!" Ruth quickly stated.

"Yes," I nodded. "Today we're celebrating an anniversary. I believe it was two years ago that you first arrived in our city. My, Neil, how you've flourished and grown since then. I recall the first time you visited our home for a story you were working on. You couldn't find your way around this town without a GPS. Now you talk like you know everyone and every street in Washington."

"Thank you," Neil said, pulling out his phone and poking at the screen. "Let me check in with my office so they know what I'm doing in case they need me. Now when you called you told me you were searching for some information? Since I still I do some writing for the police log, I'm guessing the information you need involves a crime. Correct?"

"Yes," Charlotte quickly answered. "You remember the death that occurred during the National Portrait Gallery's Gala?"

"I do," Neil nodded. "In fact, I've even written a few articles about the investigation."

"Yes," Ruth smiled, "we've noticed."

Suddenly, the sound of a bird chirping could be heard outside the cab, which was an odd sound to hear in the winter. Neil pulled out his phone, held it close to his face, and began to read something. He then started to poke his finger at the screen with great vigor.

"Give me a moment," Neil said, using both thumbs to continue to tap on the screen.

Well, that moment lasted for the rest of the cab ride. Neil continued to stare at his screen, make faces at the messages appearing, and then tap both thumbs on the screen in reply.

"For heaven's sake why doesn't he just call and talk to the person?" Ruth whispered.

"Too easy," I whispered back.

When we finally arrived at Gadsby's Tavern, we followed Neil through the front door and straight to his "favorite" table. Ruth and I smiled at each other while Neil's phone still occupied his attention. A moment later, our waitress arrived and introduced herself. Once the specials were announced, and menus distributed, Neil finally put his phone away.

"I'm sorry about that," he mumbled. "I was talking to a source about an article I'm working on."

"You mean tapping a source...I didn't hear much talking," Ruth giggled.

Neil picked up his menu and ignored Ruth's little joke.

"Order what you want, Neil," I advised, pointing at his menu. "Remember, this is our treat!"

Ruth looked at Neil and then turned to me with a grin on her face.

"You know, sister," she began, "this must be what it's like to take a son out for lunch. Of course, we never had children, Neil, but I'd imagine this is what it must be like."

Neil was nice enough to smile at the awkwardness of Ruth's sentiments.

"You know," he began while studying the menu up and down, "outside of my co-workers...you two were the first friends I made in this town. I never told you that but it's true."

"That's very nice of you to say," I smiled.

"Well, after hearing those sentiments....now I must insist that you order dessert, too," Ruth chuckled.

After studying the menu for a few minutes, Ruth and I gave Neil some recommendations from our past dining experiences at the restaurant. Soon the waitress came and orders were taken. The server was very matter of fact and quickly disappeared with our choices once the last menu was collected.

For the next few minutes, Neil, Ruth and I made small talk about the look of the restaurant, the hardwood floors and the portrait over the fireplace. We also informed Neil of the restaurant's history and famous clientele. Once light chitchat was out of the way, we decided to broach the topic that led us to extend this invitation.

"Let me begin by saying we're good friends with Webb Mills' widow," I stated. "You know Webb Mills? The man who died at the National Gallery's Gala? Anyway, Ruth and I had lunch with his widow yesterday. Of course, she's devastated. She said the police have yet to contact her about the ongoing investigation and she's really very anxious to learn more about what happened. Now I know you wrote an article about the investigation. Have you spoken with the police about this matter? Have you spoken with them recently?"

Neil took a sip of his water and looked both of us in the eye.

"Is this why you *really* invited me to lunch?" he asked, a small wrinkle forming between his eyebrows.

"To be honest, we'd been meaning to catch up with you," I jumped in, leaning forward in my seat. "In fact, Ruth and I were just talking about you the other week and I commented on how long it's been since we chatted. By inviting you here today, it just seemed like a more personal way to see you. The incident at the gala was just..."

"A catalyst," Ruth interjected.

"Precisely," I nodded, pointing to my sister.

Neil sat quietly absorbing our words before finally placing a napkin on his lap.

"What can I say, ladies," he shrugged and a smile appeared. "I work for a newspaper. I don't make a lot of money. I guess a free lunch is a good enough reason for me to sit down in my favorite restaurant and chat about a murder with friends."

I couldn't contain my relief and I smiled after hearing Neil's words.

"So, based on what you just said, it sounds like the police think it *was* a murder?" Ruth asked.

"They found a rope around a dead guy's neck," Neil said before placing his napkin on his lap. "Until they can prove otherwise, they're treating it like a homicide."

"Do they have any suspects?" I asked.

"None that I was told," Neil replied before taking another sip of his water. "From what a source told me, they checked security camera footage but it wasn't very helpful. So many people circulating around made it difficult to get a clear view of every person who entered the men's restroom that night."

"I'd imagine that it would make it difficult to identify the guilty party," I nodded.

"And what about Harlan Ellis?" Ruth asked. "Is he a suspect?"

The question took me by surprise and I cast a disapproving glance at my sister.

"What?" Ruth asked, shrugging her shoulders. "No harm in asking."

"I know you don't like him," I stated while placing my napkin on my lap. "Do you really suspect that little Harlan Ellis would be capable of murdering someone?"

"I'm entitled to ask," Ruth replied.

"Are you talking about the man who found the body?" Neil spoke up.

"Yes," I nodded.

"One officer told me in confidence they considered him a suspect...but only briefly," Neil reported.

"Why only briefly?" Ruth frowned.

"One obvious reason," Neil explained while checking his phone again. "It seems the victim stood a foot taller and weighed a hundred pounds more than that fellow you're talking about. What did you say his name was again?"

"Just call him...Lapdog," Ruth proudly announced, grinning at her sister.

"You're talking about a...dog?" Neil asked, his head whipping between me and Ruth.

"That's just a little joke between sisters," I explained, leaning back in my seat and rubbing my forehead before a headache set in thanks to Ruth. "His *real* name is Harlan Ellis."

"I see," Neil replied. "At any rate, the police decided early on that this...Mr. Ellis...just wasn't strong enough to come up from behind the victim and strangle him. Like I said, the victim was a foot taller and a hundred pounds heavier. It just didn't add up."

"Webb Mills was a big man," I nodded.

I could tell by the expression on Ruth's face she had a thought weighing her down.

"My sister and I have both noticed how Harlan's story keeps changing," Ruth finally stated with a clear direct tone. "We've attended various functions and we've heard him tell the same story over and over but in many different ways. Why don't the police pick up on that? I find that rather odd."

"They took into account those inconsistencies," Neil nodded. "In the end, my source indicated that they attributed it to old age and confusion fueled by the emotional shock of what he saw. Let's face it, ladies, old age makes everyone forget some things."

"Not us," I quickly shot back.

"Now let me tell you something," Ruth said, leaning across the table and waving her finger at our guest. "Don't make excuses for him. Harlan Ellis is not absentminded. In fact, if he saw a monarch butterfly mating with a moth, Harlan would remember how many spots the monarch had on each wing before gossiping about it. That man is a sharp as a tack and clever like a fox. The police shouldn't let him off so easily."

The second Ruth finished speaking, our lunch arrived and Neil dove right into his food. He grabbed a fork, eyed up a bowl in front of him, and began to scoop out macaroni and cheese like a child devouring candy. The food vanished from his bowl at an alarming rate. I looked at Ruth and we smiled at each other. It had been a long time since we saw someone eat with such reckless delight.

"You seem a tad hungry today," Ruth observed.

"I skipped breakfast this morning," Neil explained between bites. "I had an early meeting. I'm starving! This tastes a lot better than the usual hotdog I grab from a street vendor for lunch."

"You eat in the street?" Ruth asked.

"Oh dear," I sighed, the thought of a daily hotdog turning my stomach. "Neil, you *must* come by our house more often. We'll give you a better meal than that."

"Is it all right if we share the details of what you told us about the investigation with Webb Mills' widow?" Ruth asked. "Daisy Mills is a friend and...while I know it's not much...it is something to offer her. She's quite sad and I think she'd welcome any news."

"Sure," Neil shrugged while hunched over his nearly empty bowl of food. "I'm sure Mrs. Mills is very sad, but she's not the only one you might want to talk to. In this town, there's always someone who has an opposite reaction to a situation like this."

"What do you mean...opposite?" I asked.

Neil finished his meal in record time, shoved the empty bowl to the side and wiped his mouth with a napkin.

"I know one person who has to be very happy with what happened to Webb Mills," Neil reported. "In fact, I'd say he's probably the happiest man in Washington, D.C., right now."

"And who would that be?" Ruth asked.

"Clayton Thompson," Neil replied, before grabbing the glass and gulping down the last of his water.

Ruth looked at me and I could tell what she was thinking without a single word leaving her lips. It's the kind of unspoken connection that only the closest of sisters have.

"Why him?" I finally asked.

"I thought you ladies knew everyone in Washington," Neil laughed. "Don't you know Clayton Thompson?"

"Of course we do," I nodded. "I'm just not sure why you'd think he would be...happy?"

"According to the people I talk to, he's the only major political consultant left in town," Neil said. "From what I understand, a lot of Webb's clients have contacted Thompson about his services. His list of clients has nearly doubled in the past week, or so the grapevine is whispering. That's why I call him the happiest man in Washington D.C."

Ruth looked at me and I quietly nodded, knowing what she was thinking. In that moment, I knew we had another old acquaintance to reconnect with.

Chapter 12: Lean Days

In early winter, Washington, D.C., is stripped to the bone by the season. The garnishes of full green trees, long warm days and clusters of colorfully dressed tourists are gone. In their place, the trees can only muster dull dark branches to admire. Tourists are fewer, with only occasional school groups sprinkled around monuments. Even outdoor enthusiasts tend to retreat to health clubs rather than enduring a chilly walk, jog or ride around the Washington Monument or the National Mall. At first glance, the season truly does transform the city from a vibrant metropolis into a stagnant downtown.

However, growing up in the city, Ruth and I have discovered a silver lining to such a change. We found a counterbalance to winter's stagnation in the comfortable homes of Washington socialites. Since we regularly attend the social events of our good friends, we do notice how the cold weather brings an influx of familiar faces back to our social circles. At gatherings, we get to see faces that haven't been to a party or fundraiser in months. Faces that always seem to come back to indulge in good food and good gossip. One such face that winter regularly brings back into our social circles is Clayton Thompson.

Like Webb Mills, Clayton also makes a career for himself in the field of politics. He began on the staff of a U.S. Senator many years ago, then worked his way up to chief of staff. When the Senator retired, Clayton joined a conservative think tank where he honed his political skills for many years. Eventually, he decided he missed the political fights. That's when he started his own consulting business to manage campaigns. For the right price, Clayton Thompson will share his political wisdom with any client, as well as groom those clients who are taking their first steps into the political arena.

If you were to ever see Clayton in person, the two features you'd notice first are his slicked back white hair and his distinctive jaw. Step closer to him and you'll quickly notice how his chin slants out from his face and draws to two distinct bumps at the very tip. In my opinion, it looks like a bee has stung him twice on his chin. In addition to his hair and chin, Clayton's eyes are also quite distinctive. They're very narrow, which makes it hard to tell where he's looking when we speaks.

Over the years Ruth and I have crossed paths with Clayton at various functions. On the occasions that we have spoken with him, Clayton has always been cordial to me and Ruth. Itching to speak with him about Webb, we decided to accept an invitation to a fundraiser Clayton was throwing for a new young candidate from Florida. The invitation indicated she had her eyes on the senate. The event was being held in Clayton's home, which is a short walk from Capitol Hill.

For those of us who live in Washington, we've always known that Clayton's home is prime real estate and worth a good chunk of change thanks to its close proximity to the Capitol Building. Clayton likes to refer to his home as his "little oyster." Looking at it in passing, one would quickly notice how the home is constructed with a dull gray stone and nestled between two red brick buildings. Nothing special to look at if driving by.

On the day we arrived for his fundraiser, we stepped up to the nondescript exterior, passed through the front door and were greeted by sandy brown hardwood floors and pearl white walls. Strolling down the hallway we took in the décor, from the abstract paintings all done in light pastels, to the steel furnishings and the subtle recess lighting. It was clear from the first step into his home that Clayton was a fan of modern decor.

"I don't know whether to sit down or simply stand and appreciate the furniture as a work of art," Ruth observed.

"I agree," I nodded, glancing at an oddly shaped chair. "This isn't the kind of place one comes to relax and unwind."

Soon we heard the sound of voices fill the air. We made our way through a sitting area, where we nodded to a few familiar faces in attendance. We then stepped around a small cluster of guests before moving into the dining room.

At the center of the dining room, a long table for eight stretched out beneath a lovely chandelier that featured diamond-shaped crystal cut to maximize the light. Ruth and I excused ourselves, passing by some guests clustered around the long dining room table. We made our way into the kitchen where two chefs were hard at work and warm aromas dripped from the air.

We lingered in the doorway to the kitchen, but not because we were hungry. We both knew Clayton had a passion for cooking. As we suspected, we found him standing by a stove next to a chef. Over six feet tall, Clayton easily looked over the chef's shoulder while asking questions. Clayton gestured to a pot on the stove and the chef quickly grabbed a small container of spice and added some seasoning to the mix while speaking. Adjacent to where Clayton was standing, I saw a second chef who was working over a second range, also stirring something in a large pot. Ruth and I stepped to the center of the kitchen where we managed to make eye contact with Clayton.

"Welcome, Dupree sisters," Clayton said, looking quite happy standing between the two chefs. Clayton, who appeared to enjoy being positioned between both chefs, was very engaged in the progress of the meal. His bald head, glistening with sweat, was turning so much I thought his glasses were going to fly off. Finally, he paused, looked at us and grinned.

"Does something smell good in here, Dupree sisters, or is it just me?"

"It looks like you're giving some pointers to your chefs, Clayton," I laughed.

"These two don't need my help!" Clayton laughed. He stopped in front of us, folded his arms across his broad chest and smiled. "Now I should warn both of you that politics will be the only hors d'oeuvres served this evening. So you two better get out there and start gabbing because the main course is almost ready to be served."

"Good," Ruth smiled. "I don't know about my sister but I came with an appetite."

"Well, you have a little time before dinner is served," he continued and then he gestured with one hand to the door leading out of the kitchen. "Feel free to circulate and socialize a bit, but remember to take a few minutes to listen to my bright young candidate. She's a sharp one and the state of Florida would be lucky to have her representing them in the Senate. I value both of your opinions if you find her. When it comes to politics, you're two smart and savvy ladies and I appreciate your perspective."

"You don't have to get all sweet on us," Ruth laughed. "This isn't our first fundraiser."

"Yes, Clayton," I smiled. "You needn't worry. We brought our check book along with our appetite.

Besides, from what we've read about your candidate, the press seems quite infatuated with her. Money shouldn't be a problem to raise. Besides, we know you're always tapping the grass roots on social media for support. I'd expect you'll be getting plenty of funds for her with or without our check."

"But don't expect *us* to donate online," Ruth laughed. "We're from the old-fashioned school of politics. We'll hand you a check before we leave. We promise."

"I do not discriminate when it comes to contributions," Clayton grinned. "I take checks, cash, digital payments, piggy banks…it makes no difference to me. I'm just thrilled you two agreed to come. It's been too long, ladies. We really need to see one another more often."

"I share that sentiment," I nodded. "The last time we saw you…I believe it was still warm outside. Late last summer maybe? We were attending a performance at the Kennedy Center when we spoke with you during an intermission. Then we didn't see you for…well…it must be four months now. You just work too much, Clayton."

"You're right," Clayton smiled, his eyes glancing back to the range. "I'd like to say I'm slowing down with my age, but lately things have been picking up. Like those chefs in my kitchen…I have too many pots to stir."

"Why is that?" Ruth asked.

"It's election season," Clayton quickly replied.

"It's *always* election season in this town," Ruth laughed.

"True," he nodded, "but across the country there are many new candidates looking for guidance. They call me and I just can't say "no" to them. Lots of quality people looking to run for office. The technology these days just makes it easier to do what I do. Like I said, I'm just too busy."

"Would Webb Mills' death be another factor in having too many pots to stir?" I asked.

Clayton shook his head and his eyes narrowed.

"A shame," he quietly stated and he took one small step towards us. "I was saddened to hear of my old friend passing away like that."

"Friend?" Ruth asked. "Wasn't he your competition?"

"In one respect," Clayton nodded and he picked up a knife from a counter and wiped it with a damp washcloth. "Over the years, we ran a few campaigns against each other. However, when you do the kind of work that Webb and I have been doing...for as long as we've been doing it...you can't help but develop some mutual respect, too. No one else in this town coordinated as many campaigns as Webb and me. We developed a professional bond, along with some unwritten rules that the two of us followed regarding how we ran campaigns. Now that Webb is gone, I don't know what to expect from the young sharks who'll try to take his place. Once they devour each other, I'll know which one will challenge me. Until then, business is good...but I can't lie...it's a stressful time right now."

"Can you lend us your professional perspective on something?" I asked.

"Free of charge!" Ruth joked.

"Of course," Clayton laughed.

"As you just stated," I began, "no one coordinated as many local and national campaigns as you and Webb. With that in mind, have *you* ever left a campaign with...unhappy clients?"

"Of course," Clayton replied without hesitation. "An election is... a passionate experience, Charlotte. It brings lots of emotions to a boil. Everyone in a campaign commits one hundred percent of their heart and their passion. When a campaign loses an election, of course there are tears. Questions are raised and addressed. Candidates spend a lot of money with the expectation of winning an election. Do they have a right to be upset? I think they do."

"What's the angriest you ever saw a client get after losing?" Ruth asked.

"Let me preface this by saying I've had *many* satisfied clients," Clayton grinned.

"Of course," I smiled politely.

"With that in mind...let me think," he continued, rubbing his sharp bumpy chin with one hand while resting his other hand on the kitchen counter. "I had a few clients yell at me for a good long time. I can justify that kind of passion. Again, they put their lives and, in some cases, their family's lives on hold for a few years for the sake of a campaign. Of course, it's hard to have someone scream in your face. When that happens I simply tuck my hands behind my back, bite my tongue and hear a client out. I'm getting a hefty pay check so I tend to let my candidate take their pound of flesh from me before I move on to the next campaign."

"Have you ever had a client..." I began, but suddenly had trouble thinking of the exact phrasing.

"I believe what my sister is trying to ask is whether you ever had a losing candidate threaten to kill you?" Ruth blurted out, cutting through my hesitation with her usual directness.

Clayton's face pushed into the kind of expression one would expect to see if he found a rotten piece of fruit in his fridge.

"Just a moment," Clayton stated with a stern expression.

I watched as he turned to both chefs and waved them out of the kitchen. He followed them to the door, softly closed the door behind them, then turned and took one step closer to me and Ruth.

"I've been fortunate to lead a long life in politics," Clayton began. "A longer political life than most people should. I've worked with overachieving attorneys, perfectionist governors, mayors with sloppy morals and legislators who think they're bound for Mount Rushmore. I've heard the worst words used every which way and the worst kinds of threats you can imagine.

Never, in all my days, did I *ever* have a client attempt to do bodily harm to me, much less threaten to kill me. So, no, I don't buy the theory that's floating around social circles these days. I doubt that some disgruntled candidate got back at Webb Mills by killing him. Murdering someone...that's not evening a score for a lost election or losing time with family because of a campaign. An act like that is more personal...in my opinion."

"I see," I nodded.

"However..." Clayton began. He paused, grabbed a spoon and carefully began to stir one simmering pot.

"Yes?" I asked, feeling my body leaning towards him.

"You do have to consider those rumors about Webb's...indiscretions," he stated, staring into the pot. "Harlan Ellis was just talking about that at a party I attended the other night."

"Really?" I replied with a mock expression of surprise. "Harlan does seem to have a lot to say about this murder. Did you know he mentioned you as a possible suspect in murdering Webb? He mentioned you just the other night at a party I attended with my sister. If I recall correctly, he said your business is on shaky financial ground, which was *your* motive for killing Webb. Did he ever say that to you?"

Clayton stared at me with a steely gaze and said nothing for a few seconds.

"Of course that's all talk," Ruth shrugged. "I take everything I hear from Harlan Ellis with a grain of salt. Many people do. Don't you worry, Clayton. Nobody believes his wild accusations."

I stepped closer to Clayton and leaned one hip against the kitchen counter.

"Do you know if there's any merit to those whispers about Webb's affairs?" I asked.

"Those are old rumors," he continued. "Of course, I never witnessed anything...but those rumors about Webb's infidelities have circulated for a number of years. They've been around long before Harlan Ellis ever opened his mouth in this town. When a rumor circulates for that many years there tends to be some merit to it, in my opinion."

"And do you know with whom Webb was linked?" Ruth asked.

"I don't know any names," Clayton quietly stated. "I only know what I overheard Harlan say, which was nothing I haven't heard before. You see, ladies, you must understand that this line of work can be very demanding. The hours are long. It can be lonely. When I started finding a new romance with each campaign, that's when I decided it was only fair to divorce my wife rather than string her along with lies. Now if you'd excuse me...I need to get back to work."

When he finished speaking, Clayton pushed open the door separating the dining room from the kitchen and waved his two chefs back in. I simply smiled at Clayton, whose focus was back on his chefs and what they were doing. He had given us more than I expected. Sensing we were done, I reached for a clean spoon from an open drawer, stepped over to a pot that was on one of the stoves. I peeked inside the pot to see the source of a wonderful aroma. Inside the pot was some kind of soup. I took a deep breath and found the aroma intoxicating. One of the chefs stepped up beside me and glared at me and my spoon. He didn't speak, but did cast a disapproving expression in my direction.

"May I?" I asked, holding my spoon in the air.

The chef's dark eyes glanced down at the pot and back to me. With Clayton standing behind me, I could sense the chef was having difficulty in rendering a decision. His instinct was clearly to say "no" to my request. Yet, the expectation to please one of Clayton's guests was outweighing his instinct. Going against his better judgement, he finally offered one firm nod.

"Of course," the chef said, gesturing to the pot with one hand.

I dipped my spoon in and scooped out something that looked like beef broth with corn and crushed tomato. I blew on it once before slipping the spoon into my mouth. The spices and flavors tickled my tongue with great delight.

"Delicious," I said before dropping the spoon in the sink and ignoring eye contact with the annoyed chef.

"I'm glad the food is to your liking," Clayton observed with a measured grin.

"Of course, we're not just here to eat," Ruth spoke up. "I for one would like to meet this bright young candidate you keep talking about."

"Then follow me," he said.

Clayton led us out of the kitchen and into a parlor where he directed us to a lovely young lady standing in the middle of a group of people. With long straight dark hair and brown eyes darting around to her onlookers, the candidate gestured often with her hands while she spoke. Ruth looked at me. I looked at her. I glanced at the check book in my purse. I took a deep breath and stepped into the breech to support yet another candidate being groomed by Clayton Thompson.

Once introductions were finished I listened to her speak to me about a wide range of subjects she was passionate about. While she spoke, I couldn't help but reflect on how many times I've listened to candidates at events like this. Candidates who talk about job training, lower taxes, stronger defense, and prosperity for the middle class like they're the first ones to think of it. I stood quietly, sipping my white wine while absorbing every word she spoke, every question she answered and every smile she gave.

Later in the evening, when Ruth and I grabbed our coats from Clayton, I handed him a check. We lingered on the front stoop with Clayton, exchanging words about his candidate. Suddenly, a black bird swooped down from a nearby tree, nearly clipped our heads, then came to rest on the lamppost in front of Clayton's home. Clayton gestured to the bird.

"You see that bird?" he asked.

"The one that nearly hit us?" Ruth asked.

"Yes," Clayton said, pointing at the small black bird, which was barely visible, perched on top of the curved neck of the lamppost near the street.

"I have great admiration for birds like that," Clayton commented.

"Why?" I asked. "It's just a little bird. He's probably wishing he was somewhere warm."

"I see more to that bird," Clayton nodded. "You see, the few birds that hang around the city during the winter are what I like to think of as survivors. They could have flown south for the winter. They could have escaped to a warmer climate to live until the spring. They could have made the easy choice. Birds like that one, they stay because they know they belong here.

They choose to fight to stay here. I have a special kinship with birds like that one."

I thought about Clayton's words when we said goodbye, hailed a cab, and climbed in for a warm ride back to our home. I contemplated what he said about Webb and the rumors of his infidelities. I also thought about what he said about his admiration for survivors. Upon reflection, it made me wonder how strong Clayton's instincts really were for survival, especially when it came to his business. I couldn't believe the thought passed through me, but I began to wonder if Harlan was actually on to something? What if Clayton really was broke? Did he really need Webb's clients to survive? Ruth and I had many questions to answer.

Chapter 13: How the Heart Speaks

The next morning Ruth and I were quite content, seated at the kitchen table, enjoying our first cup of coffee, having a lengthy discussion about Clayton Thompson. It seemed like every word he spoke took us in a different direction when considering him as a suspect and whether he really had a valid motive.

Eventually, a layer of silence formed between me and Ruth. We settled into our familiar habit of having breakfast and reading the newspaper. However, we soon found that comfortable morning routine interrupted by the doorbell. Surprised by such an early caller, Ruth and I both jumped up from the kitchen table. Fortunately, we were both dressed for the day and made our way to the front door to learn who was there.

I peeked out a side window and smiled when I saw a familiar face standing on our front stoop. I quickly unlocked the door and opened it. Crisp morning air filled the hallway. My eyes focused on the visitor, but then glanced over the wrought iron fence at the edge of our small yard to another strange sight in the street. There I saw a taxi parked with a thin line of smoke trailing from the tailpipe. It appeared our guest wasn't going to be staying for very long. Ruth and I grabbed our coats and stepped outside to where Daisy Mills was waiting.

"Daisy?" Ruth said, quickly wrapping her arms across her chest. "What are you doing out here? It's freezing. Why don't you come inside and join us for some breakfast?"

Daisy stared at Ruth and me for a few seconds, then took one small step away from us.

"I can't," Daisy said. "I'm on my way to the airport. I'm going away."

Those two words took my breath away and I saw Ruth's mouth drop open.

"You're what?" Ruth asked, her head tilting slightly to one side.

"I said I'm going away," Daisy repeated, and she bit her bottom lip for a split second. "I'm leaving Washington today and you're the only two people in this city of self-important people that I've decided to tell."

I looked at Ruth. She looked at me then turned back to Daisy.

"But you've lived here for...years," Ruth quietly stated and her head briefly shook in disbelief. "Where are you going?"

Daisy stared at Ruth and her blue eyes appeared to be flickering in the morning light. When I looked closer, I saw that Daisy's eyes were actually filling up with tears.

"Oh, Daisy," I smiled, reaching out and I gently put my hand on her shoulder. "Can you please tell us what's happening?"

"I'm going back home," Daisy managed to answer, her chin quivering. "Webb and I are heading back to North Carolina later this morning. At first, I thought I'd bury him and come back here to live but...I just feel like I can't leave Webb there all alone. Not now. Once he's buried I think I want to stay with him. It just doesn't seem right for me to bury my husband and then get back on a plane for a return flight to Washington. What kind of wife would I be? I want to visit with him every day. I have so many things I want to say to him."

Daisy grew silent and Ruth's eyes drifted down, appearing to search for the right words somewhere on the ground.

"I think that's best," Ruth finally nodded.

"You see," Daisy continued, taking a small step towards us, "It feels like…every day he's been gone I just keep thinking of more things I should have said to him. Sometimes I wonder why my heart has been so slow to find the right words to say."

"The heart speaks to us in strange ways," I weakly offered.

Daisy looked at both of us, wiped a stray tear from one cheek and nodded.

"I just…" Daisy paused and drew in her breath to compose herself. "I just wanted to stop here because it was important for me to say thank you. Over the years you've both been such good friends to me and Webb. We've lived in this town for a long time and we've had our share of friendships come and go. Some of our friends died. Some of our friendships faded. Some of our friends lost elections and moved away. But you two ladies…you've been constant friends to us. It really meant so much to Webb…and so much to me."

Daisy sniffed and wiped a tear from her cheek and looked at Ruth.

"I'm going to miss our friendship," she said with a tone of voice barely above a whisper.

"Who will I go to art galleries with?" Ruth asked.

Daisy smiled after speaking and shook her head.

"Oh, Daisy," Ruth sighed and she stepped in front of me, reached out and wrapped her arms around her friend. "You know we're only one phone call away."

"That's true," I added. "When you're looking at the sunset behind those beautiful Blue Ridge mountains…and you have some memories you want to share with someone, please call us. Share them with us. We're always here, Daisy."

"I will," Daisy nodded.

She wiped away more tears from her cheeks, forced a smile, then covered her mouth with her hand as she turned and walked away. Ruth and I remained on our front porch, watching Daisy step into the street and into the back of her waiting taxi. I could feel a tear roll down my cheek after seeing Daisy in such an emotional state. Despite the cold air, Ruth and I remained on the porch and watched the taxi swerve into the street and drive away. I turned to step inside, but noticed Ruth who was still staring in the direction the taxi drove. I didn't see any tears but her expression was one of heartbreak.

"Are you okay?" I asked.

"I'm fine," Ruth answered. "Daisy's the one who lost a husband. Not me."

Together we retreated back into the warmth of our home. I went into the kitchen where I resumed my breakfast and grabbed a section of the newspaper. After a few minutes, I looked up from the paper and realized my sister wasn't joining me. Instead, a cool bowl of oatmeal and half a glass of juice marked her vacant spot.

I stood up and stepped into the hall, peeking in each room. I looked around one corner, and spied Ruth sitting in her favorite cream-colored chair in the sitting room. I could tell she was lost in thought. With her hands folded on her lap, she was staring out the large bay windows at the activity of people and cars passing in the street.

It's a place and a scene I've come to recognize all too well over the years. How many times have I seen my sister sitting in *that* chair, facing *that* window, sorting through her feelings in silence. Whether mourning a broken romance, or pondering a difficult friendship, or cooling down after disagreeing with mother, I've seen my sister in that chair many times.

When I have a problem, I tend to talk it out and share my thoughts or concerns. Not my sister. While Ruth appears to be tough and outspoken to the rest of Washington, I know there's a soft side to my sister.

Despite her comments about Daisy being the only person in this situation to feel sorry for, I began to realize that Ruth's statement wasn't entirely true. There was another person to feel sorry for. Ruth was losing a good friend. I could tell it was going to be a difficult loss for her to accept.

Chapter 14: The Social Wheel

And so it was that Daisy Mills, a pillar of Washington society for many years, quietly slipped away one morning on a plane with her husband's body. As Daisy told us, she left without seeking out attention. She left without one final gathering of her friends. She left without one word to the Washington socialites that knew her well. Instead she cloaked herself in the kind of privacy a widow usually values when grieving and headed home to bury her husband.

In the days and weeks that followed it was hard for me to comprehend not seeing Webb and Daisy's faces anymore. Not at the Old Ebbitt Grill which was their favorite restaurant. Not at any parties, which they often frequented together. Not at any fundraisers for Webb's candidates. In a town where faces changed with every election, Webb and Daisy were constants. They were a couple we could talk to from year to year and reflect on the changes in politics and the changes in the city. Now, change had found them and taken them away in the cruelest of fashions.

In response to their departure, the social scene in Washington reacted in less than sentimental ways. It never paused to mourn or reflect on Webb's death. It never stopped to acknowledge the departure of Daisy. In fact, Washington society simply continued to run like a finely tuned engine. It continued to run off the rumors and gossip about Webb's death. It continued to chatter about the possible suspects behind the murder.

Possible suspects that one Harlan Ellis freely provided at every event he attended.

Over the weeks that followed, Ruth and I continued to receive invitations to a variety of social gatherings around town. We attended various functions where a popular topic was the landscape of political candidates on the scene, which is always interesting to discuss during an election season. This was especially true for one party Ruth and I attended at a private residence in Georgetown thrown by a political fundraiser. At that event, I remember quietly walking through one room and passing by a couch when I overheard an older couple speaking quietly in a corner. I slowed my pace and I swear I overheard one of them say Webb and Daisy's names along with the word "tragedy." It was the first time I heard *anyone* in Washington society refer to Webb and Daisy's situation with any kind of sympathy, rather than scandalous innuendo.

A week later, Ruth and I were enjoying a luncheon for a retiring Representative from the House. It was at that function, packed with political figures, that I remember hearing one acquaintance actually use Webb Mills' name in a conversation. What she said took me by surprise.

"Did you hear that the young pretty girl who worked for Webb Mills has landed a job?" one woman's husky voice asked.

"You mean the tramp?" another woman's voice sharply asked.

"Aren't you being kind to call her a tramp," the first woman's deep voice hissed. "I could say worse."

The term "tramp" caught the attention of both me and my sister. It's not a word we hear very often in social settings. I turned to address the comment, then held my breath when I saw Ruth boldly step up to both ladies and interrupt their exchange. I simply shook my head and wished for the millionth time in my life that my sister could act with a little more tact.

"I'm sorry, but I couldn't help overhearing," Ruth stated, stepping between the two ladies. "Now I don't mean to interrupt you two but...I knew Webb Mills. He had many people on his staff over the years. Which person are you two referring to as *the tramp*?"

"Of course, you two know the story of what happened to poor Webb," the first woman continued, and she lit a cigarette before continuing.

"Intimately," Ruth smiled, glancing over to me. "My sister and I were at the Gala when it happened."

"Well, it seems he had a lovely young thing working for him," the woman explained, while tapping her cigarette over a crystal ash tray on a side table. "She was employed as his personal assistant up until the day he died. Her name is Sydney Sterling. She's the tramp we were just talking about."

"Excuse me," I finally spoke up, stepping beside Ruth. "My sister and I do enjoy juicy gossip as much as the next person in this town. To be honest, we're pretty thorough about most rumors circulating in this town. However, I don't ever recall hearing anything about this...personal assistant and Webb. Why would you care if this...Sydney Sterling got another job or not?"

The woman glared at me and allowed a small stream of smoke to escape her lips and twirl in the air between us.

"Because she was Webb's tramp," the woman shot back, flicking her cigarette in an ash tray on a side table. "They were sleeping together. At least that's been the rumor for more than a year now. And when a rumor lingers that long...there tends to be a hint of truth to it, my dear. I heard she got hired to staff a campaign. Anyone who'd hire a whore like that to work on their staff won't be getting my financial support for re-election."

"And who told you this...rumor?" Ruth asked.

"Oh, you know how rumors are," the woman shrugged and she reached up to the ceiling with one hand, her fingers snapping together. "They just hang in the air...waiting to be plucked. Take tonight, for example. I've heard many interesting things spoken at this party without leaving my seat. Things about people I don't even know. Now of course, because I hear it doesn't mean I know who's saying it. Isn't that how gossip works, ladies?"

With words failing me, I simply stared at the woman with a numb feeling filling my face.

For the briefest of moments, I thought I'd just met someone who was one step below Harlan Ellis in the gossip-feeding chain.

"So where do you suppose we could find this...Sydney Sterling?" Ruth asked.

"Now that's an interesting question," the woman nodded before taking another drag from her cigarette. "If you ask me, she's probably been laying low to avoid attention. From what I hear, she hasn't started her new job yet. Now from what other people tell me, she might be knee deep in packing up Webb's office. You know, Webb's wife was completely focused on burying her husband...not on the loose ends of closing up his business. From those details, I'd be willing to guess that the job of organizing the office might have fallen to Sydney."

I quietly nodded at the words and the direction.

"Did you know she was his personal assistant for seven years?" the woman continued, before burying what was left of her cigarette in the ash tray. "You can't buy that kind of loyalty in this town, ladies. They must have had a strong connection. Whether they exchanged intimacies or not is anyone's guess...but I'd be willing to wager that's why she remained so dedicated to him."

"Really!" Ruth snapped. "I happen to know Webb was happily married. We've known the Mills for several years and Webb's wife is a friend of mine"

The woman leaned a little closer to us.

"The dead have no secrets," the woman whispered, the tobacco on her breath easy to detect.

I could see Ruth's face grow red and I took her hand and led her away. Ruth spoke from her heart about Webb and his love for Daisy. However, we both knew that no man, especially an older man, could resist the charms of a younger woman. It was an old story that's been told too many times in this town. I also knew the best way to find out whether or not there was any truth to this gossip was to find Webb's personal assistant. When we left that party, we were determined to track down Sydney Sterling.

Chapter 15: Sydney

As I've stated before, Ruth and I knew Daisy and Webb Mills for many years. In that time we've been to Webb and Daisy Mills' home for a wide range of social occasions. Since we were familiar with where the house was located, it seemed like a logical place to start in our attempt to find Sydney Sterling.

We considered the home because we knew Daisy left town rather hastily, perhaps not even giving a thought to packing much of anything. We also knew Webb occasionally worked out of his home, in addition to his office. From that knowledge, we guessed that Webb might have had some work-related papers in his home that needed to be packed. Perhaps, we reasoned, Daisy would delegate the packing of those papers to Sydney. It seemed like a logical place for us to start.

Having been to the Mills' home many times, Ruth and I were very well acquainted with the building and its historical pedigree. Daisy often told us that the home had once belonged to Doctor Willard Bliss. Doctor Bliss was the physician who treated President John Garfield after he was shot. On those occasions when we attended parties thrown by Daisy and Webb, I would find a quiet corner in a room and try to imagine Doctor Bliss roaming the hallways, deep in thought, pondering how to save President Garfield from his wounds. After President Garfield died, Doctor Bliss continued to live in the home for many years, raising a rather large family in Washington D.C. Now, whether this was a story from a clever realtor or not, it is hard to know.

However, upon walking through the home during parties, I couldn't help but let my mind entertain the possibility. I often thought about how the generously proportioned rooms were probably a good fit for Dr. Bliss, his wife and their four children.

So there Ruth and I were on a cold December day, crisp winds chilling us to the bone as we stood on the front porch of Webb and Daisy's large red brick home. After ringing the doorbell, I looked up at the rounded sandstone archway just above the main entrance. While we waited, Ruth commented on the windows that dotted the front of the home, along with two French doors on the second floor that led from the master bedroom to a small balcony. I closed my fist and knocked on the front door.

"Things don't turn up in this world unless someone turns them up," Ruth mumbled.

"What did you say?" I asked, turning to her.

"I was just thinking of a quote from President Garfield," Ruth said, still staring at the house. "He once said that, "things don't turn up unless someone turns them up" and it seemed like an appropriate quote for what we're doing here. We're looking for Sydney to turn up some clues."

My sister has committed more presidential quotes to memory than anyone I know. I smiled at her observation then turned my eyes back to the unopened door before us. With no answer to my knocking, I chose to ring the doorbell again before I stepped back and looked up at the building. The door remained closed.

"This home will certainly fetch Daisy a lot of money," I observed, squinting up at the structure of the building as a whole.

"What?" Ruth asked, only half-listening.

"This house," I said, zigzagging my figure at the structure. "I think it'll sell for a nice little fortune for

Daisy. The location alone is padding enough for a good price. Besides, the age and the architecture of the building is beautiful to look at."

"What makes you think Daisy will sell it?" Ruth asked.

"Webb is gone," I shrugged, rubbing my hands together to try to keep warm. "His work here in Washington ended the day he died. There's no reason for Daisy to live here anymore. She was his anchor...but she never aligned herself socially with anyone in the city, in my opinion."

"Say what you will about her but...she was *my* friend," Ruth quickly pointed out.

"You were one of the few good friends she had, sister," I said.

Ruth reached in front of me and rang the doorbell for a third time. While we waited, a squirrel hopped down from a nearby tree and scurried across the front porch, causing both of us to jump. Despite the surprise of that little visitor we remained on the porch, our eyes locked on the door, willing it to open. Finally, I rolled up my fist and delivered two firm knocks with the help of a brass door knocker. Again, we waited. Again, no sign of anyone coming to greet us. Curious, I took one small step to my right and leaned over the iron railing to the porch to peer in through a bay window.

"Be careful, sister," Ruth advised.

Holding onto the iron railing, I managed to glimpse through one bay window where I could make out a formal dining room through some sheer white curtains, but no signs of any movement inside the house.

"I don't think there's anyone in there," I finally stated.

"Then let's get out of here," Ruth said, rubbing her hands together and quickly stepping off the porch. "I'm freezing. Let's see if we can get a taxi and warm up."

We managed to hail a cab fairly quickly and instructed the driver to take us across town to the Union Trust Building, where we knew Webb's office was located. Just a block away from Lafayette Square, the high-rise is close to our home. If it weren't for the brisk weather, Ruth and I would have preferred to walk from the Union Trust Building back home rather than paying for another cab.

"Oh, how I do miss taking walks on warm days," I sighed to myself as we arrived.

Climbing out of the taxi, the white stone high-rise was hard to miss. Built in the early 1900s, the structure was originally a bank. Over the years, Webb Mills kept his office there from the first day he arrived in Washington. While other professional occupants came and went, Webb remained loyal to the location and the view of Lafayette Square from his office.

We moved under the rounded archway that marked the main entrance. Once inside, Ruth and I took the elevator up to the top floor where we walked down a narrow hallway with cream-colored walls and lavender bead board paneling. Eventually we stopped at a nondescript door with a frosted window at the center. There was no name on the glass and no sign around to designate the space as belonging to one of Washington's most influential political operatives. For all the years he was there, Webb never bothered to identify his office with a sign or a nameplate.

"It is hard for me to believe that a man like Webb could shape the country's political landscape...yet refuse to have his name on the door of his office. A nice man who was humble to a fault, in my opinion," I observed.

"You know what he told me?" Ruth recalled. "He said, "Ruth, a name on the door doesn't matter one lick.

If someone wants me bad enough they know my phone number." I'll never forget those words."

After sharing that memory, we heard movement coming from inside Webb's office. It sounded like shoes shuffling across hardwood floors. The sound grew louder and softer again. Through the frosted glass pane, I could see a figure moving behind the door. I reached down and grabbed hold of the door knob. When I turned it, I realized that the door was already open a crack. I pushed it open wider and found a desk at the center of the office with a pile of boxes stacked around it.

"Hello?" a woman's voice called out from the back of the room.

Ruth and I looked at each other.

"I'll have more boxes ready for you in a minute!" the woman's voice instructed from somewhere. "You can start with that pile by the desk. I already marked which ones go into storage and which ones go to Mrs. Mills."

"Excuse me," Ruth called back. "I think you're mistaken. We aren't the movers!"

With that one statement, I heard the sound of heels tapping loudly on the hardwood floor. Out from behind a stack of boxes, a young woman's head poked out. She was shorter than me and Ruth and looked to be a few decades younger. Her hair was platinum blond, pulled back in a tight bun, like a ballerina. Her face was pale, which drew more attention to her bright red lipstick. She wore a black sweater with the sleeves pushed up to her elbows and a pair of jeans that hugged her lean physique. Her head tipped to one side when she made eye contact with us. She quickly approached, heels tapping the hardwood floor with each step.

"I'm sorry," she smiled. "Can I help you? Are you two ladies lost?"

"We're not lost," Ruth said, looking around. "As a matter of fact, we've been to this office many times over the years."

The comment caused the young lady to put down a folder she was holding and step closer to us. I could tell by the look on her face she was confused.

"We were friends of Webb Mills," I explained.

"Oh," she said, her head tipping to one side. "I am…I mean I was…Mr. Mills' personal assistant. My name is Sydney Sterling. If you're here to see him, I'm afraid I have some bad news for you ladies."

"We know what happened to Webb," Ruth said.

"We were at the National Gallery that night," I nodded. "Such a tragedy."

"Yes, it was," Sydney said, her dark eyes glancing back and forth between us.

"As my sister implied, we've known Webb for a long time," I stated and stepped up to Webb's desk and ran my hand across the top of it. "I remember how fond he was of this office. He used to tell us that he loved the view. He often said he enjoyed looking at Lafayette Square from his desk. He called it his 'patch of peace in a whirling city.'"

"How did you know him?" Sydney asked, taking one step closer to us. "Did he run a campaign for one of you?"

Ruth and I both laughed.

"Heavens no," I smiled. "Let's just say we were constant friends in a town where people came and went after every election."

"And how about you?" Ruth asked. "Did you work for Webb for a long time?"

"Yes and no," Sydney smiled. "If you counted calendars, then yes, you'd count a lot of years. If you're asking me if it *felt* that long to me, then I'd say no. You see, Webb hired me right out of college. I went from living in a dorm to being swept up in his world. As his personal assistant, Webb took me everywhere with him."

"That must have been exciting for a young girl like you," I smiled.

"It was," Sydney nodded. "I did trips around the country and visited cities I'd never been to before. I even met celebrities. When I look back, I guess I found the life Webb introduced me to quite intoxicating. I liked working for him. In fact, I used to tell Webb I'd never leave him. I'd tell him the only way he could get rid of me is if he'd leave me. In hindsight, I guess that was a rather prophetic thing to say."

I watched Sydney as she turned and looked out the window, taking in the view of Lafayette Square. The same view Webb admired when sitting at his desk. She slowly crossed her arms in front of her waist and took a deep breath.

"You know, whenever he left the office at the end of the day," she continued, "I could always count on him to say three words. He'd always say, "See you, Sydney," before walking out of the office. I'd hear it every day. I could count on it the way I could count on the sunset. It happened so much I just took it for granted. Oh, how I'd give anything to hear him say those words to me one more time."

She turned away from the window, looked at us and offered a half-hearted smile while nervously tugging at the sleeves of her black sweater.

"It's been a difficult loss for us, too," Ruth said.

Sydney looked down at the floor, grabbed an empty box and placed it on the desk.

"If you'd excuse me," she spoke at barely a whisper, "it's a big office and I have a lot more packing to do."

I stood there watching Sydney pull open another drawer, remove more files, and carefully place them in a box. She marked the outside of the box before securing the lid with packing tape. Watching Sydney resume her work, I could sense that our discussion had come to an end. Ruth and I quietly slipped out the door leaving Sydney to continue her work.

When we got home, Ruth and I found our cats looking quite lazy. Oliver was stretched out on the hallway floor by a vent where warm air was pouring in. Mezzo was curled up on a chair in our sitting room, tail snapping against the cushion. I walked into the kitchen and grabbed a carving knife from a drawer. I picked up an apple from a bowl, sat down at our kitchen table and began to carve the red skin from the apple. With each careful slice, I reflected on our glimpse into Webb's office and our chance meeting with Sydney.

"Layers," I mumbled to myself, while slowly removing the apple's red skin.

"What?" Ruth asked, sitting at the kitchen table.

"This murder," I replied, while accumulating a ribbon of red peel on the table. "This whole situation...I just have a sense that there are many layers to it, sister."

Ruth pulled out a chair and sat down at the kitchen table with me. I handed her a slice of my apple before carving another slice for myself.

"That girl, Sydney," Ruth sighed, turning the apple slice in her hand. "I just can't believe how much she looks like a younger version of Daisy Mills. I wonder if the two of them ever met? If so, I can only imagine what Daisy thought of her? It's like looking into the past. No wonder Webb hired her and kept her on for so long."

"Well, we know what Harlan has been saying about her," I stated. "After meeting her for the first time, what are your impressions, Ruth? Do you think Sydney loved Webb? Do you think they were sleeping together?"

Ruth slipped the rest of her apple slice into her mouth while considering the question.

"If she was having an affair…I would have expected to see more emotion from her?" Ruth observed. "She seemed relatively composed, in my opinion. Somewhat chatty. Very courteous. Certainly focused on the task of packing Webb's office."

"I would have also expected more tears from her," I commented. "At the very least, I'd expect her to get more emotional about her recollections…if they were lovers. After all, as we saw with Daisy, a woman's heart needs solace. Daisy simply left town without even saying goodbye. *That's* the behavior that reflects a broken heart, in my opinion."

"I agree," Ruth nodded. "She was too matter-of-fact for me, sister. Grieving certainly does not include…packing boxes and sharing memories about flying around the country with a smile on your face."

"Although people do grieve in different ways," I pointed out, before slicing away the last piece of apple from the core.

"You know, when we were at Olivia Parson's home for tea the other day I overheard that Lap Dog talking again," Ruth began.

"You mean Harlan?" I interrupted.

"If that's what you prefer to call him," Ruth grinned. "Anyway, I overheard him at this party and he was telling a small group of guests that he knew for a fact that Sydney was indeed having an affair with Webb. He then quickly concluded, in his overdramatic way of course, that Sydney must have killed Webb in a lover's rage since he wouldn't divorce poor Daisy. Now, having spoken with Sydney, do you see her being someone who could muster up that kind of rage? Can you imagine her choking the life out of Webb…or anyone else for that matter? That's not the kind of person we just met, in my opinion. She didn't seem to have that...passion to me. Besides, she was *very* petite."

"And we both know Webb was a big man," I nodded. "I doubt she could have choked him to death. Besides, how could she slip in and out of the Men's Room without drawing attention? Someone would have spotted her."

"The Ladies Room is very close," Ruth pointed out.

"Lots of people passing in and out of both bathrooms," I nodded. "Very difficult to sneak in."

"What if she wore a disguise?' Ruth suggested.

"Perhaps," I mumbled, lost in my thoughts.

"I checked and she *was* at the event," Ruth nodded. "I spoke with a friend at the National Gallery and Sydney's name was on the guest list."

"Being Webb's assistant, I'd imagine she was always by his side," I sighed.

We both grew silent. I stood up and tossed the apple core in a garbage receptacle. I walked back to the table, grabbed the carving knife, then returned to the sink.

"Getting to the truth of this matter is going to take hard work, sister," I advised while washing the carving knife and placing it back in the drawer. "We have a lot of loose ends to pursue. I think we'll need to be in a lot of places over the next few days. There are lots of people we need to talk to if we want to get to the truth about Webb's death. There's no doubt in my mind it'll be hard work."

"Well, you know what Woodrow Wilson once said," Ruth grinned and she pointed one finger up in the air. "He said, "The man who is swimming against the stream knows the strength of it." I believe we're about to start swimming against the stream, sister."

I leaned my hip against the kitchen counter, folded my arms and grinned at my little sister and her well-chosen words.

"You are truly a quote machine," I laughed. "I've been giving it some thought this afternoon and I think I know someone who might be able to make our swim a little easier."

Chapter 16: One Glimpse

Kitty Sweeny is one of those people whom Ruth and I enjoy seeing at social events. A short slender woman with plain features and an infectious laugh, Kitty blends in with a crowd. On those rare occasions when our paths cross, Ruth and I often find ourselves seeking out Kitty and exchanging stories with her about how Washington D.C. used to be compared to how it is today. I find it delightful to share memories with someone who can appreciate the recollections of Washington when the city was more cordial and less divided by political lines.

Kitty is around our age, and is one of the few acquaintances we know who has lived in the city nearly as long as we have. Like us, she was born and raised in Washington social circles. Unlike us, Kitty married at an early age. Her husband died in his forties in a car accident, which was quite a tragedy for Kitty to bear. Widowed at a relatively early age, she never felt the urge to remarry and remained a widow for nearly five decades.

Aside from going through life with a broken heart, the thing that I find fascinating about Kitty is her brutal honesty. In a city where people would rather talk around an issue, or bend the truth for the sake of a vote, Kitty has never altered the facts to spare a person's feelings.

No matter what the event or whom she socializes with, Kitty is always brutally honest with what she says and how she says it. With that quality in mind, I invited

Kitty to our home to have a conversation about Webb and those long-standing rumors of his infidelities. If there was anyone who could shed an honest light on the rumors about Webb and Sydney's relationship it would be Kitty. Of course, finding Kitty was hard to do. She's a busy woman with a packed schedule of engagements with friends. It took us a few days to finally reach Kitty and a few more days for her to work us into her schedule.

Sipping hot tea on a cloudy winter day is a pleasing way to spend an afternoon. It's like sunshine in a cup. This was especially true on the day we finally welcomed Kitty into our home. After making small talk about the chilly weather, our cats, and our home, Ruth lost her patience with my topics of conversation. Right after I served Kitty a steaming cup of earl grey tea, Ruth jumped the gun and explained our real motives for inviting her to our home.

Before I could interrupt, Ruth went on to present Kitty with the details to those long circulated rumors of Webb's indiscretions. After hearing Ruth speak, Kitty paused for some silence to ponder her next words carefully. She took a calculated sip from her tea cup. She delicately placed the cup back on her saucer and placed it on the coffee table before us. She looked at both of us and smiled. Kitty could sense Ruth's eagerness to learn the truth and savored every second before parting her lips to speak.

"You two have known me long enough to realize my words on matters like this are as good as truth," Kitty began. She leaned forward in her seat and turned her eyes to me. "Would you please pass the sugar, Charlotte?"

I quickly did as she asked. Sitting on the edge of the sofa, I passed a small crystal bowl of sugar to Kitty.

Ruth, seated in a chair next to the couch, was also leaning forward. Together we watched, with our mouths hanging open, as Kitty carefully scooped a spoonful of sugar into her tea cup and stirred it. She picked up the tea cup, took one sip, and nodded at her taste buds' response.

"Now where were we?" she asked, sitting back with her tea cup cradled in both hands.

"We were discussing Webb Mills and those rumors," Ruth answered.

"Ah, yes," Kitty nodded before taking another long sip of tea. "Now what I'm about to tell you is something I witnessed with my own eyes, ladies. It happened a few months ago. It's something I haven't shared with anyone simply because no one ever asks me questions about Webb Mills and his fidelity to his wife."

"So...what did you see, Kitty?" I asked, sensing my eyes growing wider.

She stared down in her tea cup for a moment before looking at us.

"I saw *him* with another woman," she began before looking back down into her cup.

"Webb?" Ruth asked.

Kitty offered a silent nod in reply before carefully putting her tea cup down on the coffee table.

"When? Where?" Ruth asked, her voice growing anxious. "I...I can't believe it!"

"What I saw occurred at a restaurant called Plume," Kitty continued. "It's a small establishment here in the city. Have either of you been to Plume?"

"No," Ruth replied.

I simply shook my head.

"Oh, ladies, you must go," Kitty grinned. "It's a restaurant buried deep in the confines of the Jefferson Hotel. It's one of those hidden gems, which is part of its charm. If you go there, you'll find it to be a lovely little place. The décor is elegant with white walls, colonial touches, discreet lighting, and a fireplace that, when lit, provides an extra layer of intimacy to the dining experience."

"Sounds lovely," Ruth nodded.

"Plume is quite the draw for D.C. couples to escape," she continued and then paused for a little smirk to appear. "I'd like to say mostly married couples go there but a few husbands come when they discreetly leave their wives at home…if you know what I mean."

She paused again to allow her lips to curl up a little higher beneath her cheeks.

"Of course," I smiled back.

"So one evening, I thought I'd take my granddaughter there to celebrate her promotion at work," Kitty recalled. "During the course of a wonderful meal, I excused myself to go to the powder room. I walked by a few tables then noticed a closed door off to one side. It was a door I knew led to a private dining room in Plume called the Wine Room. It's a spacious private dining area usually granted to VIPs who wish to eat in private. Of course, I was curious as to what famous person was eating in there. So when the server cracked open the door to go inside the Wine Room I had to sneak a peek. That's when I saw him."

"Who?" Ruth asked.

"Webb?" I asked.

She nodded and looked at both of us.

"Yes, there he was sitting with that young girl he employs as his assistant," she recalled.

"I recognized her platinum blond hair. In those fleeting seconds before the door closed, I could see him holding her hand, his other arm draped around the back of her chair. They were close together and they were both smiling. It was only for a second or two but...it was enough of a snapshot for me."

I was stunned by what I just heard.

"I can't believe it," Ruth managed to say.

"Now, like you two," Kitty continued, "I've known Webb Mills for many years. It was the first time I ever saw him in a situation like that. Over the years I've gotten so used to seeing him with Daisy and *only* Daisy. I never saw him in the company of another women until that night. I actually tried to go to his office the next day to confront him about what I saw. When I was greeted at the office by the same young lady...I simply turned around and left."

"Sydney," I whispered to myself.

"You know that tramp's name?" the woman asked.

I glanced over at my sister. Her mouth was hanging open after hearing all the details.

"Perhaps they were having...a staff meeting," Ruth weakly suggested.

"People don't hold hands at staff meetings," I pointed out.

"Despite knowing Webb and Daisy for many years," Kitty continued, "I have to admit that this development came as no surprise to me. I mean...take a man, give him power, let him hire a young thing who has looks and brains and, of course, he's going to get weak and eventually do something stupid. How many times have we seen *that* same story play out in this town, ladies?"

"Too many times," Ruth said, her voice barely above a whisper.

Kitty paused and her eyes drifted to the floor.

"It's like putting the bird cage next to the litter box," Kitty laughed, pointing to our cats on the floor. "You know sooner or later something bad is going to happen."

"I agree," I replied, the image of Harlan yelling about a murder at the National Gallery Gala flashing in my head. "Something bad *did* happen, Kitty. Someone was murdered. Ruth and I need to know how and why."

Chapter 17: Motto for a Guest

I've always thought that Russell Strickland, Russ to his friends, bears a striking resemblance to Ernest Hemingway. With his slicked back salty white hair and a neatly trimmed beard that extends down the sides of his cheeks and around his chin, Russ projects the image of a distinguished politician to anyone who meets him. Yet, those in certain Washington circles know Russ as something far more important than a political figure. He is a natural resource that most every political figure in Washington seeks out to meet.

The natural resource Russ brings to Washington is money. He is that rare combination of a generous donor who likes to keep a low profile. I would imagine that Russ Strickland is a name on the phones of most every politician in D.C. While he never makes the news, or seeks the spotlight, it is well known in political circles that Russ cuts more checks during election season than anyone else in D.C.

However, Russ is not just an open bank for candidates to tap. In fact, he is very meticulous about the candidates he supports and the causes he champions. Ruth and I thought there was a good possibility that some of Russ's candidates were defeated by Webb Mills' candidates. If so, it only seemed logical to ask Russ for any names of disgruntled candidates he may have supported. Specifically, candidates with an axe to grind with Webb Mills.

So after our meeting with Kitty Sweeny, my sister
and I decided to invite Russ Strickland to our home for
a Sunday lunch. Of course, we scheduled our meeting
earlier in the day so as not to miss out on a Washington
Redskins football game. My sister and I were raised to
support the team by our father, which meant we were
taught at an early age to always be loyal and to never
miss a game. Despite our investigation, we knew the
team was in need of a win and desperately required our
support, not to mention our lucky football we rub
before each game.

With that in mind, Russ arrived to see us on a chilly
Sunday afternoon. He came with light snow falling over
the city. We watched him cut up the snow-covered
walkway, his steps leaving marks on the thinly-covered
path leading to our front door. Watching it fall from a
side window, the snow reminded me of ticker tape one
would see slowly descending on a parade. The poor
weather conditions didn't seem to dim Russ's spirits.
When we greeted him at the door, he flashed an easy
smile the second he stepped into our home.

To be perfectly honest, we didn't just invite Russ
Strickland. We lured him. We told a little white lie by
implying we were curious about a candidate he was
supporting. Knowing we had deep pockets, not to
mention a mutual love for Washington Redskin
football, Russ was quick to respond and quite jovial
when he entered our home. I could tell he was thinking
he was about to enjoy an afternoon with friends who
shared a love for football and were going to agree to
drop a big check in the pocket of a candidate he was
supporting. Unbeknownst to Russ, nothing could be
further from the truth.

"I must confess I'm actually excited to be here,"
Russ grinned, handing me a thick black winter coat and

matching leather gloves. "After all, it's not every day the Dupree sisters extend an invitation to me."

"Don't take it personally," I smiled. "At our age we tend to accept more invitations than we give out, Russ."

"It's too much fuss for my sister to entertain," Ruth complained. "Not me. I'm always ready for a party."

The remark caused Ruth to laugh leaving me to nod in agreement. Ruth has always been the social one, while I tend to be more introspective in my preparations for entertaining a guest. While Ruth will focus on food selections and cleaning the rooms, I'm always giving more thought to the topics of conversation and the interests of the guests we invite.

"Whatever the case...it's a delight to see you both," he smiled, before glancing out a window. "Only during election season would I make a trip across town in this kind of weather. Usually I'd be sitting by my fireplace, sipping cognac from my favorite snifter glass while reading a good book."

He rubbed his hands together as he followed us into the sitting room. Once seated he crossed one leg, stroked his full white beard and let his eyes take in his surroundings.

"My how this room is bright," he grinned. His head turned and he nodded at what he saw. "The white walls. The cream-colored chairs and couch. The off-white throw rug over the hardwood floor. All nice touches. And those windows really let in the natural light. A delightful room, ladies."

"Thank you," I said. "This is our favorite room in the winter. In fact, it's our favorite room for entertaining, too."

"Speaking of entertaining," Ruth began. "How many candidates have you met with this year, Russ? Like you said, it is a busy time with elections and all. Are you supporting anyone?"

"I'm broke!" Russ joked with a hearty laugh. "I think I'm supporting too many candidates. I've met lots of good candidates choosing to run in what I would call a reactionary mid-term election. Of course, that's just my opinion."

"How so?" Ruth asked.

"I see this election as a strong response to our newly elected president," he continued. "The country wants balance and they always support the minority party in mid-terms. The only problem is that nothing is gonna get done when they do that. The days of bi-partisanship are long gone if you ask me."

"So who are you supporting?" I asked.

"I'm supporting getting things done in Washington," Russ explained, sitting up a little straighter. "We need our Congress and the President to be on the same page for some important issues. That's why I'm supporting the President and I'm supporting his party."

The statement caused my eyes to roll over to my sister, who was already looking back at me with a slight scowl that I recognized but our guest did not.

"How...patriotic of you," Ruth smirked, a hint of sarcasm in her voice.

He looked a bit surprised by her comment and her tone.

"Russ, we've known each other for a number of years," I began. "You know we didn't invite you here to sit in our home and watch you dance with your words. Let me cut to the chase. We know the bulk of your investments are in real estate. They always have been. We also know your other favorite kind of investment is in candidates that you feel will support your interests. All very legal. So don't sit there and talk to us about your loyalty to the president...unless you expect us to stand up and pledge the flag with you, too."

Russ looked at me, his eyes squinting together and his lips forming a half-smile.

"I think I understand," he replied, looking a little shocked at my bluntness.

"We just want you to be more forthright when you speak," Ruth advised.

"My sister is right," I said, my voice growing more relaxed. "We're all old enough to wear our honesty on our sleeves, Russ. We don't need to slip on social graces this afternoon. Besides, in this house we have a motto for our guests...tact won't get you tea or biscuits. Both of which, I might add, are in plentiful supply today."

The comment caused Russ to break into a gentle, almost polite laugh.

"Point well taken," he smiled.

"Now that we've established some rules...may I ask a direct question?" I inquired.

"Of course," he nodded, again stroking his beard.

"We know you tend to invest a good deal of money in supporting your candidates," I began. "Sometimes when my sister and I give a few dollars, and a candidate loses, we feel a bit shortchanged by the whole process. Have you ever had that feeling, Russ? Have you ever lost too much money on a candidate you were supporting? I don't need exact numbers...but I'm just curious about the candidates you thought were going to win...and didn't. How much did it cost you?"

The question caused Russ to look up in the air and remain silent for a moment. While we waited for an answer, I watched our cat, Mezzo, enter the room and curl up on the floor by the fireplace. Russ finally looked at me and appeared to have collected his thoughts.

"Let me preface my answer by saying...it doesn't happen very often," he began.

"Of course not," I smiled, knowing full well my reply was meant to stroke his ego.

"With that in mind, there was this one candidate a few years ago," he said. "He was a representative from Arizona, who had an eye on the Senate. I don't remember his name but...he was a real hot-head but a gifted orator. It took me tons of money and time to meet his demands and get him to support some new real estate bills I had my eye on. Despite his temperament, he really was a natural on the campaign trail. Once we had an understanding, I thought I picked a real winner. Come election day the polls were in his favor and he was looking like he would win. Then, as sometimes happens in elections, the people's vote went against him. He lost and I was out a good chunk of change."

"Was he upset about the loss?" I asked.

"Absolutely," Russ laughed. "I told you that guy was a hothead. Of course, that was a few years ago. I don't even know if he still lives in Washington anymore. You know how it is in the House...too many representatives to keep track of from one election to the next."

"Do you remember who ran his campaign?" I asked.

"He brought in some fella from Arizona with no experience in managing an election," Russ explained, and then he just shook his head. "Looking back, I think it was a cousin or second cousin or something. Anyway, the kid was a lawyer but didn't know squat about campaigns. Webb Mills was running the other campaign. Webb torpedoed the new guy's campaign right out of the water in the last months of that election."

"Webb Mills?" I asked.

"Yeah," Russ nodded. "Webb used some strategy to get the candidate caught between releasing his financial statements and claiming they were private. When the guy finally refused to release the records, Webb's candidate quickly jumped in and said his opponent had something to hide. Then Webb's campaign pivoted and turned it into a character issue. In the end, Webb pulled out all the stops and his candidate won easily. For the life of me, I can't think of the name of that hot head who was running against Webb and his candidate."

"Does the name Wendell Cremins sound familiar to you?" Ruth asked.

Russ's eyes grew wide and he waved his finger at my sister with great vigor.

"That's the guy!" he said loudly. "You just read my mind, Ruth Dupree! How did you know what name I was thinking about?"

"I heard the name from a little lap dog I met at a party last week," Ruth grinned.

"A talking dog?" Russ replied, half-smiling. "I...I don't understand."

"Forgive my sister's humor," I said. "She's talking about a friend of ours who likes to gossip a good bit. His name is Harlan Ellis."

"I know that name," Russ nodded, pointing at me. "He's the fellow who found the dead body at that gala the other week. From what I understand it was quite a traumatic experience for him."

"He'd be the first to tell you as much," Ruth smirked.

"Forgive my sister's sarcastic tone but there's a curious nature to what Harlan has been saying," I grinned. "It seems he remembers a different killer every week. At this party, it was poor Wendell Cremins who was being implicated by Harlan. The week before that it was someone else. Even right after the murder Harlan blamed the widow for killing her husband."

"I guess it could be anyone," Russ shrugged.

"I don't suppose you'd know where we could find this...Wendell Cremins?" I asked.

"Like I said...it's been years since I spoke with him," Russ explained.

"Well," I said, sitting back in my seat, "this is one of those times when it's a benefit to belong to Washington Society, Russ. One well-placed phone call should get us what we need."

Chapter 18: Refreshments

Ian Walsh was getting tired of listening to Charlotte's story. She could tell by her guest's narrowing eyes that he was getting a bit fatigued by every detail she was conveying. Also, his perfect posture on the couch had gradually transformed into a slumped position. Yet, as Charlotte knew, there was no short answer to Ian's query. He wanted to know why the review of his meal for the National Portrait Gala was bumped from the newspaper. It was a complicated answer. She had many details to share regarding what happened that night and she wasn't about to leave anything out. Charlotte stood up and smiled at her weary guest.

"Let's take a break, shall we?" she suggested, stepping in front of Ian. "Can I get you something to drink? Would you like to walk around and let us show you the rest of our home?"

"I'm fine," Ian shrugged, raising his arms in the air and stretching. "Just a glass of water would be fine. I am a little thirsty."

"Let me go get some for you," Charlotte said, before disappearing into the hall.

The second Charlotte stepped out of the room, Ruth quickly picked up the remote and turned on the TV. An emerald football field illuminated the screen and the cheers of fans filled the room.

"Do you watch football, Ian?" Ruth asked while staring at the screen.

"Sometimes," Ian replied, checking his phone and ignoring the TV. "Most Sundays I'm usually catching up with scheduling meals for clients for the upcoming week. Lately, it seems to be the only day of the week I'm able to catch up on things. Every once in a while, I'll go out and treat myself to a breakfast on a Sunday. The way I see it, at least there's one day out of the week when someone is gonna be in a kitchen preparing a meal for me. I do like football, though. I wish I had more time to watch it but work comes first in my life."

Ruth nodded at the comment, leaning forward in her seat.

"Charlotte and I never miss a game when Washington is playing," Ruth replied, her eyes still locked on the screen. "It looks like we're ahead for now."

She smiled when she noticed that her guest had put down his phone and was also staring at the screen. A roar from the crowd caused her eyes to turn back to the screen.

"Sister," Charlotte said, entering the room. "We have a guest visiting. Why would you turn on the TV? Please turn it off."

She handed Ian a glass of water, then quickly glared at Ruth, giving her the kind of displeased look that only a little sister could interpret. To appease her big sister's sentiments, Ruth turned off the TV and mumbled something under her breath before turning to Ian.

"So this Harlan Ellis character," Ian began. "He sounds like a tricky fellow to me. I mean if he's always exaggerating when he talks to people…how can you tell what parts of his stories are true and which are lies?"

"I agree with you, Ian," Charlotte said. "He is a very tricky fellow. Let me tell you a story. The first time I met him, Harlan Ellis told me he was born in Valdosta, Georgia. Now at that time he didn't know I had a sister.

So at the very same party, when he crossed paths with Ruth, he introduced himself and told her he was born along the coast of Norfolk, Virginia."

"A complete fabricator from the get-go," Ruth chimed in.

"Not the best first impression," Charlotte sighed.

"I see," Ian nodded. "So...that Wendell Cremins fellow...did you ever find him? You know, the guy with the bad temper from Arizona. He sounded like a good suspect to me."

"The beauty of being well connected in Washington society," Charlotte grinned, "is that we knew the number of a good friend to call. Friends can be so helpful when it comes to matters such as this."

Chapter 19: How That Man Could Talk

In order to find Wendell, I made a phone call to
North Carolina and chose to ask Daisy about the man
Russ was directing us to. When we finally reached her,
she was surprised to hear our voices. I held the phone in
between us so my sister could hear. It was good to
listen to Daisy's voice again. After some catching up
and polite chitchat, I could sense it was time to get to
the heart of the matter.

"Daisy," I began, glancing at my sister, "do you ever
remember Webb talking about a man named Wendell
Cremins? He worked in the House of Representatives."

"I remember the name," Daisy quickly answered.
"From what Webb told me, Wendell was quite the
storyteller when it came to stump speeches. In fact,
Webb used to say that Wendell fancied himself to be
the second-coming of President Ronald Reagan. During
the campaign season, he would really embrace
Reagan's knack of storytelling on the campaign trail as
a way to engage voters, or so Webb told me. I believe
he was running for a senate seat, but Webb defeated
him."

I saw Ruth closing her eyes and rubbing her
forehead.

"Are you okay, Ruth?" I asked.

"Hearing that comment about presidents who like to
tell stories just brought back a painful memory," Ruth
said and she started to rub the sides of her head.

"What memory do you mean?" I asked, pulling the
phone back.

"I just had a painful flashback of a long-winded storyteller we met many years ago," Ruth said.

"Who was that?" I could hear Daisy's voice ask through the phone.

"What Daisy said reminded me of the time that father introduced us to President Lyndon Johnson for the first time. Do you remember that, Charlotte?" Ruth recalled.

"Oh yes," I nodded.

"What about Lyndon Johnson?" Daisy's voice asked over the phone.

"If memory serves," Ruth recalled, "it happened in the winter at a holiday performance in Ford's Theater. After a rousing show by a military band, father made eye contact with the President on the way out of the theater. If I close my eyes, I can still see President Johnson, dressed in a tux, waving us over with a big smile. Of course, the Secret Service was none too pleased, but I guess we looked pretty harmless, two high school girls and their father."

"I do remember that," I nodded and pointing at Ruth. "Long after everyone was gone, our father and the President continued to chat."

"Yes," Ruth nodded. "If I recall correctly, Johnson had recently moved into the role of President and was asking father about the state of the economy and seeking advice on some legislation that he was crafting."

"Why your father?" Daisy asked over the phone.

"I don't know," Ruth replied. "We were teenage girls caught up in our lives at that age. I remember how father was well respected in political circles back then, but I was never sure why. Looking back, I'd suppose Johnson was seeking advice from lots of people he respected, including father. So after a few minutes of picking father's brain on a wide range of topics,

Johnson finally noticed us standing next to father. That's when he were introduced."

"That's right," I nodded. "I always thought President Johnson was a nice enough man, but he sure could talk. I remember how he started off by quizzing us about what colleges we were going to attend. Of course, we gave him the names of a few east coast colleges that mother and father had mentioned. With each college we cited, I noticed that President Johnson's eyes began to squint together and his head shook in a disapproving manner. When we were finished listing our prospective colleges, Johnson stepped between us and our father and began to speak at great lengths about the benefits of colleges in Texas. For the longest time, he went on a lengthy tangent about how wonderful the colleges were in his home state, how warm the weather was, and then a number of stories about his experiences going to school at Texas State University. He ended his speech by recommending we should come to Texas because it would be a wonderful adventure for two sisters like us."

"And of course," Charlotte chimed in, "he's making eye contact with us the whole time so neither one of us dared to look away, or even blink for that matter. I mean....it was the President. By the time he was finished, my eyes were burning."

"Indeed," Ruth said. "I don't know about Ronald Reagan but Lyndon Johnson...*he* was a *real* storyteller."

"Well," Daisy's voice chirped over the phone after listening to us droll on. "I don't think Wendell Cremins is *that* bad but he can go on a lengthy tangent if you let him. He likes to talk."

"Do you know where we can find him?" I asked.

"I believe he's still buried in the House with all those other representatives," Daisy sighed. "If memory serves, he must be starting to plan his campaign for re-election and looking for donors."

"Along with every other candidate in Washington," Ruth mumbled.

"There's one other thing I remember Webb told me about that man," Daisy continued over the phone. "Aside from being long winded, Wendell also has a reputation for having a short fuse. Webb told me that Wendell has the highest turnover rate of anyone in the House of Representatives when it came to his staff. Now Wendell's supporters will say he has a high standard for his staff. The critics say he verbally attacks his staff for the slightest of reasons and that he does it too often. Do you think he may have something to do with Webb's death?"

"When we speak with him we'll let you know," I answered.

"And how do you think we'll get the chance to see a representative during an election season?" Ruth jumped in with her question. "He's going to be way too busy for us."

I tapped my purse and winked back at my sister. She looked at my purse and a mischievous grin slowly appeared. One of the many joys of having a sister are those moments when words aren't required to read each other's thoughts or finish each other's sentences.

Chapter 20: Cremins

The next morning, my sister and I braved the chilly weather and took a cab to Capitol Hill with hopes of finding Wendell Cremins. After walking around the halls of the U.S. Capitol Building, we got lucky and spotted Representative Cremins and his staff. Trailing behind him for a few minutes, I think the best way to describe Wendell would be to imagine the Scarecrow from the Wizard of Oz racing around Capitol Hill like he drank nine cups of coffee.

With a full head of thick white hair, Wendell is rail thin with a brisk stride and an animated way of speaking. All of those details were on full display when my sister and I spotted him. He was surrounded by five younger staff members and was filling the hallway with his booming voice. The group, as a whole, were sharply dressed—the men in navy blue suits, and the women in navy blue pants suits.

We trailed behind Wendell and his staff through some lengthy halls on the way to his office. We noted how he spoke to some members of his staff with loud bursts of suggestions and questions. We also could see Wendell waving his hands while he spoke, almost karate chopping the air in front of him after every sentence. I saw one young lady desperately trying to type on her phone while listening to Cremins along with maintaining the fast pace that the group was setting.

"He acts like he's the center of his universe," Ruth observed.

"And his staff certainly does do a good job of letting him think so," I replied.

Ruth and I followed behind at a safe distance, letting Wendell lead us through many hallways and directly to his office. When his pace slowed at one door, and I saw the door swing open, I knew we had arrived.

"This way, sister," I called back to Ruth.

Together we followed him through the doorway and into a cramped office space where I noticed one staffer quickly break away from the pack. Wendell and the rest of his staff stepped behind an open door that I assumed was his private office. The lone staffer left behind turned around and blocked us from following Wendell any farther. The staffer was a young man who looked like he was closer to being a teenager than twenty. He stood his ground while Ruth and I stared him down.

"May I help you, ladies?" he asked, gesturing with one hand for us to stop.

"We have an appointment with Representative Cremins," I said, pointing to my watch.

I stared at the closed door leading into Wendell's office while the young man took three quick steps across the cramped office space to his desk. He pointed one finger down to a notebook on his desk and leaned over it the way a mother bird checks on its babies in a nest.

"What are your names?" he asked.

"Charlotte and Ruth Dupree," I replied.

He raised one finger and glanced back down at his desk. I was surprised to see him pick up a pair of reading glasses from his desk and slip them on his youthful face. He dipped his head closer to a notebook and appeared to be studying its contents. A few seconds later, he nodded, looked up and focused on us.

Despite the reading glasses, his boyish appearance reminded me of myself when I was recruited to work for a representative right out of high school. While I wasn't sure of this young man's age, I could only guess that he was in the same age range. I could also understand the weight of responsibility being given to such a young person.

"I see your name right here," he reported, glancing up at us with a smile.

"Splendid," I replied, leading Ruth by the desk and towards the door that Wendell had stepped through.

"Wait!" I heard a voice call out.

Again, the young man danced out from behind the desk and stopped in front of us.

"Now I'm afraid that Representative Cremins is running a little late this morning," he quickly explained. "You see, ladies, he just returned from a committee meeting and I'd like to give him five minutes to clear his head before I let him see you. He can give you maybe ten minutes before his next committee meeting."

Ruth glared at the young man and I could tell she was trying to remain calm over the terms he was dictating.

"Very well," I smiled and simply folded my hands in front of my waist.

The young man smiled and went back to his desk.

"He has some nerve," Ruth whispered in my ear. "Shouldn't that *boy* be playing high school football instead of giving us terms to follow for our appointment?"

"Hush!" I replied, checking my watch. "It's only five minutes."

Having worked for a Representatives as a secretary, I was a bit more understanding about the young man's request. When I was employed as a secretary in the House of Representatives I was barely nineteen and had just finished high school. Despite my youth and inexperience, one of my jobs was to guard my boss's office like a hawk on more than one occasion from visitors. Whether they were well-meaning constituents or fellow representatives, I kept them away from my boss whenever he asked me to. In fact, I can even recall turning away one very friendly representative from across the hall who liked to pop in unannounced.

He was a nice fellow from Michigan who liked to drop by the office on Mondays to shoot the breeze with my boss about football. His name was Gerry and there were some days when I knew my boss was simply too busy to talk with Gerry, so I'd turn him away. Years later, everyone in the country knew Gerry by a more formal title, President Gerald Ford.

After exactly five minutes, according to my watch, I noticed Cremins' office door swing open and some of his staff slipped out. I then saw the young man stand up from his desk, smile at us, and open the door to Representative Cremins' private office.

Upon entering the office, I was impressed at the size of the space. While the outer office area was cramped, Cremins' private office was quite spacious. A hunter green rug spread across the room, with maroon leather chairs and a matching couch near the door. At the back of the office, I spotted a window directly behind a large oak desk where Cremins was seated. Judging by the size of his office, it was clear to me that Wendell had served many terms to work his way up to such an impressive space. Newly elected representatives would drool to be given an office with such impressive dimensions.

When he saw us, Wendell quickly stood up from behind his desk, stepped around and greeted us the moment we set foot through the door. He gave both Ruth and me a vigorous handshake and smiled with the kind of ease that a seasoned politician would use during election season.

"Good morning, Dupree sisters," he grinned. "When I saw your names on my schedule today I knew it would be the highlight of my day. Such a treat to have the famous Dupree sisters here."

Ruth and I looked at each other, a bit confused by his words.

"I don't believe we've ever met before," I finally said.

"That's true," Cremins stated while shaking my hand again. "However, your reputation does precede both of you. When I mentioned your appointment to a couple of colleagues in my hallway yesterday, they told me how influential you two are in this town. A couple of jewels in the social scene, or so you were described. So…I'm honored to have you both here today."

"Jewels?" Ruth giggled, turning to me. "I don't think I've ever heard us described like that, sister!"

"It is a kind sentiment," I said to Ruth before turning to Wendell. "I'm glad you heard only good things from your friends, Representative Cremins. You see, during election season we tend to support some candidates but we also pass on supporting quite a few, which angers some people. Campaign season is a process we're quite familiar with. You see, we were born and raised in this town so we've seen many candidates come and go, which is why we're so selective in whom we support."

"I can only imagine the people you've met and the history you've lived through,"

Representative Cremins sighed while shaking his head.

"Well…we're old but we didn't pay for George Washington's campaign!" Ruth snapped.

The comment caused me to shake my head at the words coming out of my sister's mouth.

"Oh...I didn't mean to comment on your age," Wendell quickly apologized.

"Don't mind my sister," I smiled with a wave of my hand. "I'm afraid the years have taken a toll on everything but her vanity."

The quip brought Wendell's easy smile back into view.

"So how can I help you two?" he asked, tipping his wrist up once to check his watch.

"I don't know if you realized it, but we were anonymous donors when you ran for the U.S. Senate a little over a year ago," I lied, and I followed up that lie with the sunniest smile I could muster. "Now we've been hearing rumors that you may decide to run again for the senate. If so, we'd like to offer more financial support to you. We also have a network of wealthy donors who could also provide additional financial support, if you need it. Now, of course, your re-election campaign for your current position comes first. We understand that. Assuming you win, which I'm sure you will, how would you feel about making another run for the Senate?"

Representative Cremins grew silent. For the first time all day, this man of perpetual motion actually grew quite still to consider my question. He reminded me of a deer frozen by the headlights of a car. His eyes turned from me, to Ruth and back again.

"The idea of running for the senate, well, let's just say that ship has sailed," he finally spoke, slipping his hands into his pockets while glancing out his office's window.

"How so?" Ruth asked.

"When I first ran," he observed, "the people in my district knew me, but the rest of the people of Arizona didn't. To them, I was like this new car you see at a dealership, all shiny and sharp and ready to go. So a lot of people in Arizona came out for my rallies because they were curious about me. They come out to look under my hood and kick my tires, so to speak. I loved getting to meet new people and travel around my home state."

"It sounds like you enjoyed the experience," Ruth observed.

"In the beginning I did," he nodded. "Now my opponent was less congenial about his campaign. In fact, he let his campaign manager go quite low…personally and professionally. That's why I lost my bid for the senate."

"You could always run again," Ruth suggested.

"It's not that easy," he sighed before dropping into the leather chair behind his desk. "You see, my opponent's campaign manager lifted up my hood to the people of Arizona. He showed them all of my political flaws. I'm afraid, you just don't recover from an experience like that. Voters these days, they want their candidates perfect…not human. I'll be lucky if I get re-elected to another term here in the House."

"Terrible," Ruth sighed with a sympathetic voice.

"That sounds like a nasty election you went through," I observed, knowing full well that Webb Mills was the campaign manager for his opponent. "You must have been quite upset by everything they did to you."

"I'll tell you what really steamed my beets was when they made an issue about my dog!" Cremins stated with a voice that grew sharper and louder. "Because my wife and I chose to buy our dog, Buster, from a breeder instead of going to an animal shelter, my opponent made THAT an issue! Can you imagine? Even my own dog lost me votes?"

"How underhanded!" Ruth snapped.

"Dirty politics!" I joined in.

"Yes...it was," Cremins stammered, his eyes blinking quickly. His face looked flushed. He grabbed a pen from his desk, nervously tapped the tip of it on the desktop, then drew in his breath and smiled. "So like I said...my ambitions for a Senate seat are in the past. No plans on doing that again."

His face was flushed and he made a fist with one hand and pounded it on his desktop. It sounded like a hammer hitting the desk and it made Ruth jump.

"All because of the pond scum who ran that campaign!" he grumbled. "Thanks to him I'll probably have to get rid of my dog to get re-elected."

Ruth and I looked at each other.

"That election was nearly two years ago," Ruth pointed out. "Plenty of time for the voters to change their minds about you...and your dog."

"Yes," I said, nodding at my sister's words. "I agree. Listening to you, I get the feeling that this loss is still very painful for you."

"I'll be the first to admit it's taking me a while to get over," he nodded.

Wendell took a deep breath, checked his watch, then abruptly reached across his desk and shook both of our hands.

"Thank you for offering your support, ladies," he said standing up, his voice returning to a normal volume. "I'm afraid I have a committee meeting to get to and I need to review some notes. Perhaps we can meet again? Maybe over lunch some time?"

"That would be nice," I smiled, knowing the invitation wasn't because of our good looks but our potential for donating money to him.

"Check at the desk and my staff will set something up," Wendell advised before slipping on some glasses and directing his eyes to a small pile of papers on his desk.

I thought his invitation to be a half-hearted gesture. Ruth and I stood up and I turned for the door when I noticed my sister was still standing in front of his desk.

"May I ask you one final question?' Ruth asked.

"What is it?" he asked without looking up.

"Did you ever meet with Webb Mills about running such a disgraceful campaign strategy?" Ruth asked.

The words caused Wendell to look up from his paperwork. He removed his reading glasses and glared at Ruth. His eyes narrowed and he slowly leaned back in his chair.

"How...how did you know Webb Mills was the one who ran that campaign?" he asked.

"If there's one thing you should know about us," Ruth replied without hesitation. "We have lots of friends who like to talk. We know everything that happens in this town."

"Better than the Internet," I smiled.

Wendell Cremins let out a sigh and checked his watch again then tucked one hand on the leather belt on his hip.

"I never spoke with Webb after that campaign," he answered, his eyes turning back to his desk, as if the memories were scattered somewhere in the papers spread across his desk. "To be honest, I never once thought about doing it."

"Why wouldn't you confront him?" I asked.

Wendell glared at me.

"Because I flush turds down the toilet," he coolly replied. "I don't dignify them with phone calls."

"You do know he's dead?" Ruth asked.

"I read that," he nodded, putting his glasses back on and shifting some papers to the center of his desk. "I was at the gala that night. I heard Harlan Ellis carrying on. That's when my wife insisted on leaving. Harlan's yelling and the things he was saying upset her. As luck would have it, we managed to duck out just before the police arrived."

"So you were with your wife the whole evening?" I asked.

Wendell quietly nodded.

"We both would swear on a stack of bibles to that," he replied, standing up and stepping towards the door. "My wife and I have been churchgoers all our lives, ladies. So, for us, putting a hand on a bible and taking an oath isn't something we take lightly. I talked to Clayton Thompson, too. He'd vouch for me. Besides, if I wanted to kill someone I certainly wouldn't do it in a room where there are people around. I'd pick a less populated place. Doesn't that make sense?"

I nodded at his logic.

"Now if you'd excuse me, I really must get going or I'll be late," he said, slipping on his suit coat before charging out of his office. Ruth and I watched him leave, then noticed a small familiar face appear from the side of the door frame. It was the young man from the desk.

"You two may also leave," he grinned.

The cab ride home was a quiet one. The morning sun was low in the sky, casting golden light that flickered between some buildings. I adjusted the wool scarf around my neck while Ruth fiddled with her gloves.

"Should we contact the wife?" Ruth finally asked. "I can make some phone calls and get her name."

"I don't think that'll be necessary," I answered.

"Why?" Ruth asked.

"Because I don't think he killed Webb," I slowly replied, my eyes staring out the window.

Silence fell between us again. Ruth nervously tugged at one of her gloves. I could sense my sister was in disagreement with my sentiment.

"In talking to him, he still seems very angry about that election," Ruth observed.

"No one likes to lose," I pointed out.

"Yes," Ruth countered, "but it's been two years. Two years! You don't see me pounding my fist on a table with all my might because of something that happened two years ago."

"Be that is it may, let's look at the facts," I replied. "He was with his wife at the gala."

"Or so he says," Ruth countered.

"I think she would have noticed a change in him if he strangled someone," I pointed out.

"I mean, only a sociopath would be able to murder someone and then return to eating his dinner while acting normally around his wife and other guests. Besides, Cremins is a representative. You don't keep a job like that by being mentally unstable. He's in the spotlight with his staff and his constituents. If he had a psychological disorder, it would have been noticed by someone long before that gala. The job requires too many meetings and too much interaction with people. He might be angry but…I don't think he's unhinged."

"Then who are we looking for?" Ruth asked.

"I think the person we're looking for is someone filled with rage," I suggested.

"Someone who's so angry they'd be crazy enough to kill Webb with a room full of people just a few steps away. Representative Cremins isn't angry enough or crazy enough to do that."

Ruth turned and looked out the cab's window at the morning traffic going by.

"I do find all of this very hard to imagine," Ruth sighed.

"What part?" I asked.

"Here's what I keep thinking about," Ruth began and she cleared her throat before gathering her thoughts.

"You and I go to a lot of social events every year. We attend a good many galas and fundraisers and luncheons. Whenever we go, we tend to see the same faces and we talk to them about the same topics. It's like being part of a club, right?"

"Agreed," I nodded.

"Over the years," Ruth continued, "we've even gotten to form some really good friendships and some good acquaintances in our social groups. We have a sense of the people we socialize with from all the gatherings we've attended together. When I think about those groups, it's just hard for me to imagine that one of those people...maybe even a person we know quite well...could be capable of being a murderer."

I nodded at her sentiments. I never thought about it, but Ruth was right. It was hard for me to imagine that the face of the killer could very well be a face that we both knew as a social acquaintance or even a friend.

"You're right, sister," I said, turning my eyes out the cab's window. "When we get down to the truth I think it might be hard for us to come to grips with it. We know a lot of people who attended that gala. It will be difficult to imagine one of them being clever enough to hide their rage behind a pleasant smile and proper manners.

"Apparently, it's not that hard for Harlan Ellis to imagine," Ruth grinned. "The way that man runs his mouth he's already implicated half the town in Webb's murder."

"He does seem to be getting a lot of pleasure out of Daisy's tragedy," I nodded.

"It makes me mad," Ruth grumbled.

"Then perhaps we should do something about that...lapdog," I suggested.

Despite the dark interior of the taxi, I could hear Ruth giggling from her side of the seat.

Chapter 21: The Harlan Effect

For the better part of a week, Ruth and I began to make phone calls, chat at social events and review invitations we received. We put our social antennas out and quickly filled our calendar with a wide range of engagements. Then, I did something that made my little sister quite upset. Once we had a healthy amount of invitations, I explained to Ruth that we were only going to accept invitations to events that we knew Harlan Ellis would attend. Of course, my sister found this criterion quite hard to swallow. She began to debate the merits of my strategy with me. While she spoke, I turned on some classical music, sat down on our fluffiest couch in the sitting room, took a deep breath and tried to act like the mature sister.

"We're cat people...we don't care for dogs...especially lapdogs!" Ruth snapped, again referring to her nickname for Harlan. "You really expect me to endure *him* for a week or two? I attend social events to have a good time, not to get upset by the ramblings of a liar."

"Sit down beside me, take a deep breath and hear me out," I answered in the calmest voice I could muster.

Once she did as I suggested, I began to lay out my plan. I stated the obvious, we needed more details about the night of the murder, not to mention the scene of the crime. I also reminded her that, like it or not, Harlan Ellis was the only one to witness the crime, or so he said. Finally, I presented her with a simple fact...the larger the crowd the more Harlan liked to talk. He simply adored being the center of attention. By attending the same social gatherings as Harlan, and eavesdropping on his dramatic recollections, it seemed like a sound way for us to identify some good facts to work with. After a lengthy period of silence, my sister reluctantly agreed to my plan. Of course, getting Ruth to agree was the easy part. Lining up and attending one social event after another was going to be the real challenge.

The first occasion we had to catch up with Harlan Ellis came at the home of Evelyn Rhine. A member of the Washington Ballet Board of Directors, Evelyn was hosting an afternoon tea to discuss plans for the annual Washington Ballet Gala, which was about six months away.

Once everyone had arrived, Evelyn situated herself on a couch in her spacious sitting room and held court over her guests. Nestled between four of her closest friends, two on either side, Evelyn began to address those in attendance and explained her ideas for the gala. Once she finished, and asked for thoughts, the other guests expressed a wide range of views about everything from flowers, to food, to music. Most suggestions were discarded by Evelyn, who had a clear notion of what she wanted to do. While everyone in the room kept their attention on Evelyn, I kept my eyes on Harlan.

I noticed how he would look at Evelyn and nod at all the right times, especially when she spoke or made eye contact with him. I also noticed how he only sipped his tea twice during the first hour and how he commented on the delightful flavor of the tea whenever Evelyn asked. With all due respect to the hostess, I didn't learn much about the gala she was planning, but I did discover that Harlan was not a fan of tea by how little he sipped and how much he left in his cup. I also came to the conclusion that he was an excellent liar, based on the expression he mustered before complimenting Evelyn on the quality of her tea. The same tea that, from what I observed, he never drank and eventually dumped into a potted plant.

Eventually Evelyn wrapped up her meeting, leaving small clusters of guests to mingle and discuss matters while she excused herself to her spacious kitchen where she wrote down some ideas that agreed with her. Looking at the guests mingling around the main room, I quickly drifted into a corner chair, leaned forward in my seat, and began to listen to Harlan describe his ordeal over finding Webb's body to a small cluster of ladies around him.

"You know, I practically tripped over the body," he gasped, his sad eyes circling around at the guests surrounding him. "I mean, there I was minding my own business when the killer practically knocked me down at the entrance to the bathroom. Well, I was lucky to keep my balance after that collision. Then when I did get into the bathroom I nearly dropped over when I saw this hulking man's body lying dead on the floor just outside of the bathroom stall. It was a horrible sight to behold for sure."

"And how did you know he was dead?" I asked, getting out of my chair.

Every head surrounding Harlan turned in my direction.

"Excuse me?" Harlan replied, scanning the room. "Who asked that?"

"I did," I said, raising my hand like a school girl addressing a teacher. I stepped closer to where he was seated and cleared my throat. "Now you just said you nearly fainted when you saw the dead body on the floor. I was just wondering how you knew he was dead in the few seconds you had walked into the bathroom?"

Harlan glared at me and the expression on his face told me the question was not welcome. Sitting there with a foul look on his face, I thought Harlan looked like an elf in need of an enema.

"Could you speak up?" Harlan asked, his bushy white eyebrows pushing together.

"How did you know the body on the floor was dead!" I asked with a louder voice.

"The man had a rope around his neck so I just assumed he was," Harlan stated.

"Were there any marks, or bruises, or cuts on him?" I asked.

"I didn't take the time to inspect the body," Harlan quickly replied. He turned around to the faces listening to him and then he looked at me. "I was in shock. I ran out of the bathroom once I saw him. I didn't stay to examine it. Now if you don't mind, Charlotte, you're interrupting my story. These people would like me to continue. Am I right?"

I turned my eyes to four white haired ladies and one young man standing around Harlan. The ladies appeared to be my age, each holding a different expression that made them appear like children listening to a bedtime story. The young man was listening while poking at his phone.

"Let him speak," one of the ladies finally said.

Harlan looked at me and a small grin appeared on his face. It was the kind of grin that I remember the Cheshire Cat having from an old *Alice in Wonderland* book mother used to read to us as young girls. The illustration of this particular character fit Harlan's expression to a tee.

"My apologies," I said with the calmest voice I could muster. "By all means, please continue with your account of those events, Harlan. I didn't mean to interrupt."

I quietly stepped back behind Harlan's groupies and let him continue with his account of the events. While he spoke, I caught a glimpse of Ruth in an adjoining room.

She was comfortably seated on a ruby red couch, holding a plate of food on her lap, looking quite happy as she nibbled on a few hors d'oeuvres. When Ruth made eye contact with me, I waved her over but she simply pointed at the food on her plate and shook her head. With Harlan filling the air with his theories about who he thought killed Webb Mills, I quickly made my way across the room.

"It's your turn to listen to him!" I snapped.

"What?" Ruth asked.

"I said it's your turn to listen to him!" I said again, rubbing a throbbing temple on the side of my head. 'He's talking about the murder again. Hurry and get over there."

"No," Ruth grinned before crossing one leg and leaning back in her seat.

"I've been stuck there for two hours and I'm getting hungry," I complained, pointing in Harlan's direction.

"Forget it," Ruth laughed, before taking a bite of a cracker with what looked like crab meat on it. She pointed at me and grinned. "This was *your* idea, sister. Not mine. Listening to that high-pitched lapdog for that long…I'm not surprised your head hurts. As a matter of fact, I'm surprised it hasn't just exploded right off your shoulders by now."

In spite of my empty stomach, and a borderline headache, I couldn't help but laugh at my sister's comments. I glanced over my shoulder at Harlan, then quickly grabbed my sister's plate full of food and took it from her before I walked away.

"Hey!" she called out.

"Back to work!" I said before charging back across the room, nibbling from Ruth's plate of food while listening to Harlan ramble on.

Two hours later my stomach was full but my ears were ringing louder than they were before the party. When I typically go to socialize, I like to move around, picking and choosing interesting people to listen to before going off to a quiet room or corner to reflect on the conversation. While I felt an obligation to stay close to Harlan and his many thoughts about Webb's murder, part of me was longing for a quiet corner to reflect on everything I had heard...and to soothe my headache.

When it came to suspects, Harlan implied that Daisy was the murderer, as he had done at other parties. From eavesdropping on Harlan at a number of social engagements, I did hear him change his accusations more than once. Sometimes the killer was Daisy. Sometimes it was Webb's personal assistant, Sydney Sterling, followed closely by the belief that Sydney and Webb were having an affair. He also pointed the finger at a rival campaign manager, Clayton Thompson, on one occasion. Even the disgruntled Representative from Arizona, Wendell Cremins, was accused and given a reason by Harlan. At one event, Harlan even suggested that the person who bumped into him at the Gala may have even been a killer for hire. With so many of Harlan's theories to consider, it was quite challenging for me to stay focused on the facts, rather than his long list of suspects.

On a chilly Thursday night in December, Ruth and I found ourselves arriving at our next event to spy on Harlan Ellis. For this occasion, Ruth and I were driven to the suburbs of McClean, Virginia, for a lovely little get together thrown by Hugh and McKenna McCall.

The McCalls are from England and, as the story goes, they met many years ago while working on the staff of the Prime Minister. Having talked to them at various social affairs, Ruth and I have often commented on the McCalls and their delicate voices, refined manners, and lovely accents when they speak. I find their manner of speaking quite pleasurable to listen to. The reason for the social event they were hosting was to introduce their oldest daughter to the social circles of Washington D.C.

It was a lovely affair with an extensive list of guests from the most prominent families in the D.C. area. Ruth and I were surprised to see so many familiar faces in one place. Their daughter, Rachel McCall, was all of twenty-two years old. When she stepped into the room for the first time, her long dark hair flowed over her shoulders and down the back of an emerald dress that was cut just below her knees. Elegant yet not too formal, in my opinion. When I stepped closer to introduce myself, I thought it was no coincidence that the satin fabric of Rachel's dress matched the color of her eyes.

"Do you remember when mother did this for us," Ruth whispered.

"I do," I smiled back. "She was quite proud to show us off."

"Like a couple of horses being trotted around to prospective suitors," Ruth joked.

"Yes," I nodded, "she dressed us up and took us around to everyone. Although, looking at Rachel, she seems to be enjoying it all a bit more than we did."

I stood in the corner and watched Rachel's parents, both in their sixties, escort her from one room to the next, presenting their daughter to the most influential people of Washington society. At every introduction, Rachel flashed a smile as bright as any summer sun before charming guests with her pleasant demeanor. Her fiancé, a young lawyer from one of Washington's oldest firms, stood in the back of the room grinning at the activity. His thick black hair was combed to the side. His hands were tucked in the pockets of his tan slacks while a navy blue blazer covered his broad shoulders. His handsome smile reflected a man who was comfortable to blend in with the other guests on this day, leaving Rachel to do the socializing.

Of course, I kept one eye on Harlan while the McCalls circulated around the party with their daughter in tow. At one point, I held my breath when I saw the McCalls introducing Rachel to Harlan.

"Here we go!" my sister whispered in my ear. "Another reason for him to start up with that story again."

Surprisingly, it was the only moment of the evening when I saw Harlan open his mouth and not speak of Webb's murder. Instead, he simply smiled, introduced himself, and commented on the lovely dress Rachel was wearing. He made a little joke about his white hair and his age, shook hands with Rachel's fiancé, then wished both of them well on the rest of the evening. It was a polished performance by Harlan, allowing the spotlight to remain on Rachel McCall. However, as the evening wore on, I knew Harlan's old instincts would begin to get the better of him.

After leaving the room to seek out a drink, and chat with an acquaintance, I returned to find Harlan sitting on a couch with a cluster of guests standing around him. He loudly spoke about his near brush with death at the National Portrait Gala, as I expected. I felt a hand nudge me in the back. I turned around to find Ruth standing behind me.

"Step closer," she urged.

"Would you like to listen to him this time?" I asked, pointing in Harlan's direction.

"No!" Ruth quickly replied, stepping back and grinning at me. "This was your idea."

"Please, Ruth!" I begged, rubbing my eyes. "I'm tired and I don't want to get another headache like last night. You know how I went straight to bed when we got home."

"This was your plan, so see it through," Ruth explained while settling into a rocking chair. "Now you already sat through his stories more than once this week. All you have to do is listen to him again so you can pick out any discrepancies in what he mentions. Hopefully you'll pick out what facts from his story have changed and what facts remain the same. If I listen...I won't know the difference."

I rubbed my forehead and thought I felt a headache coming on. I glared across the room at Harlan and took a deep breath. Unfortunately, Ruth's thinking made sense. I shook my head at the prospect of spending yet another party hanging on every word Harlan spoke. I tried to keep my composure. I grabbed my sister's arm and pulled her close.

"The least you can do is get me a plate of food while I'm shackled to him!" I grumbled.

Ruth allowed a small grin to curl up her cheeks.

"I'll be happy to drop by with some food throughout the evening," she said before dashing off. "Enjoy the lapdog!"

I made my way across the room, sat down on a couch not far from where Harlan was speaking to a cluster of guests and I tried to focus on every word. This time, I sat with my back to him so I didn't have to make eye contact and create a mock expression of interest. After numerous gatherings, I was growing tired of watching his small face change and contort to

underscore the dramatic nature of every detail. Instead I
stared at the fireplace and enjoyed the licks of flames
that flickered in and around some logs. From where I
sat, I began to listen to every word Harlan spoke as well
as his overly dramatic tone.

"So you didn't see the killer?" I heard one woman
ask.

"That's like asking if you saw the wind?" Harlan
quickly replied. "You know, I was walking near
DuPont Circle the other day and when I turned a corner
that north wind just came out of nowhere and hit me
full blast. It actually pushed me back a few steps when
it hit."

He clapped his hands together for dramatic effect.

"It practically took the hat right off my head," he
continued. "That's what it was like walking into that
bathroom at the National Gallery. One second I'm
minding my own business. The world as I knew it was
quite normal. The very next second I turned that corner
to head into the bathroom...and bang! I get run over by
a vicious killer and the world changed!"

Then Harlan smacked his hands together again for
dramatic effect, causing one lady sitting beside him to
jump so much she nearly spilled her coffee.

"Could you make out the killer's face, Harlan?"
another woman asked.

"I'm afraid I couldn't see very well because of the
poor lighting," Harlan explained. "After the killer
knocked me over, I knew that, whoever it was, he or
she was in a hurry. When I finally managed to get to
my feet and step into the bathroom I saw the dead body
on the floor. That's when I realized why that person
was in such a rush to leave and why they plowed me
over the way they did."

"So what did you do?" a women's voice asked.

The voice posing that question made me curious. I turned to see that the source of those curious words was none other than Rachel McCall. She stepped between two older ladies and stopped right in front of Harlan. She was so close the tips of her shoes were nearly touching his shoes.

"I don't know what I'd do if I saw a dead body," Rachel stated. "What did you do, Mr. Ellis?"

For a moment, I thought Harlan looked a bit perplexed. Perhaps it was due to Rachel's appearance, or her question, or both. He paused for a moment, his mouth open a crack and his beady brown eyes centered on Rachel while he stewed over how to respond.

"Well, my dear, anyone who was at the gala that night will tell you I responded by running out of that bathroom screaming murder!" Harlan replied, his high-pitched voice growing sharper by the end of the sentence.

"So you ran into the killer, but you couldn't tell if it was a man or a woman?" Rachel asked, her head tipping to one side.

"That's right," Harlan sighed.

"Did you at least smell anything?" Rachel pressed. "Did that person say anything to you? What kind of shoes were they wearing? If they knocked you to the floor I'd suspect you'd at least be able to catch a glimpse of their shoes."

I turned and smiled at Rachel. I was growing to like that girl with every question she asked. She stood in front of Harlan looking perfectly innocent, hands folded in front of her lovely dress, her emerald eyes locked on him for an answer. It was clear to me that the neurons in her young brain were firing on all cylinders. She wasn't satisfied with just being entertained by Harlan's story. She was ready to slice up his tale and dissect every part of it.

When I turned to look at Harlan's face it held a bright shade of red. His eyes kept flicking between Rachel and his audience and I was curious to see how this was going to play out.

"Well? Did you or didn't you see the killer's shoes?" Rachel repeated, folding her arms across her chest while her eyes narrowed. "Please, tell us, Mr. Ellis. I'm sure I speak for everyone here when I say we want to know every detail. Did you see the killer's shoes?"

Harlan's eyes grew twice their size and his face was flushed like a tomato. Despite sitting on the other side of the room from the fireplace, he nervously dabbed at the sweat on his forehead with the back of his hand. Just when I was enjoying watching Harlan squirm, Rachel's mother appeared out of nowhere. Dancing around a group of people with the grace of a hummingbird, she grabbed her daughter by the arm and gently pulled her away from Harlan.

"Come here, Rachel!" the mother quipped. "I have someone I want you to meet."

With his inquisitor safely removed from the scene, Harlan let out a sigh and slumped back in his seat. He gestured to a server for a glass of red wine and then proceeded to drink half the glass in a few gulps. He turned to his left then his right to the older ladies on either side of him and sighed again.

"Where was I when that rude young lady interrupted me?" he grumbled before taking another healthy sip from his glass. "No manners on that girl, if you ask me."

One woman reached out and began to rub his shoulder to soothe his hurt feelings.

"There, there, Harlan," the woman seated to his left said. "She's young and full of curiosity. She clearly doesn't understand the trauma you've been through."

"Yes, Harlan," the older woman seated to his right nodded. "She's young and not as sensitive as you are."

Both ladies continued to stroke Harlan's ego with kind words and attention. He sipped more wine from his glass while absorbing everything they said, occasionally nodding in agreement. When the compliments subsided, he lowered his glass and smiled at the sweet words being offered by the sympathetic ladies around him.

"Thank you," he said to them, finishing the other half of his glass of wine with one quick swig. "Now, where was I with my story?"

"You were telling us about the moment you stepped into the bathroom," one lady replied. "You said it was hard to see before you went in."

"Oh, yes," he nodded, pointing at her. "So there I was entering the bathroom. And what a horrible sight awaited me. It only took me a few steps to find the body and I actually gasped when I saw it. Now...I don't think I've ever gasped in my life but I literally made this sound."

And he placed his hand on his chest and inhaled with a wheezing sound.

"That's what I sounded like when my eyes came to rest on that corpse lying on the bathroom floor right next to the toilet. Why...that poor man didn't even have time to flush before he was attacked."

That, I thought, *was a new detail I didn't need to hear.* The notion of being strangled right after going on the toilet certainly painted a picture that was too vivid for my taste.

"Now, of course, the person who ran into me was a tall person," Harlan recalled. "I know I'm only about five feet tall, and everyone looks tall to me, but this person was clearly in a hurry and strong enough to knock me right to the ground."

"They committed a murder," the lady on Harlan's left observed. "Of course they were in a hurry, Harlan. They were fleeing the scene of the crime."

"That's what I think," Harlan squeaked, pointing at her and nodding his head.

"You poor dear," a lady on his right mumbled.

"So who do you suppose that person was?" the lady on Harlan's left asked.

"That's where it gets tricky," Harlan replied. He sat back in his seat and cradled his glass of wine with two hands. "You see, I've been trying to merge who I ran into with who I think killed Webb Mills. A jealous wife? A jilted lover? An angry candidate who hired Webb and then murdered him in a rage over a lost election? Perhaps, even, a certain political rival who is making more money with his consulting business since the murder. I've considered many suspects since that night but I just can't think of which one I had actual physical contact with."

Harlan didn't have to mention any names with his accusations. Every person in the room was knowledgeable enough to know which individuals he was talking about. I took a deep breath and tried to control my temper after hearing him throw poor Daisy into the mix. She was newly widowed. She didn't need a veil of suspicion hanging over her, too.

"Or perhaps some angry, deranged person hired an individual to kill Webb Mills," Harlan shrugged. "I may have run into an international assassin without even knowing it."

After hearing those claims, I found myself reaching for a second glass of wine from a passing server. I sat comfortably for the rest of the night, next to the fire, drinking while I listened to Harlan's squeaky voice go on about his international assassin theory.

As the night wore on, it made me angry that Harlan failed to utter one kind word about the victim or his widow. In Harlan's mind, *he* was the victim, not Webb and Daisy Mills. There were plenty of opinions I overheard but few facts revealed on this night. Once again I was subjected to another dramatic narrative about Harlan coping with his shocking experience, but few facts to hang my suspicions on. It was another night ending with two aspirin to remedy yet another headache.

Chapter 22: Another Occasion

Two days later, Ruth and I decided to attend the National Press Club's luncheon. The National Press Club has been in existence since 1908. Over the years it has hosted various heads of state, as well as newsmakers, to address its members on a wide range of issues. The group even has its own emblem, the owl, which embodies a journalist's wisdom, habit of working long nights, and awareness. Comprised of mostly journalists, the organization hosts about seventy lunches a year that anyone in Washington is able to attend for the right price.

The guest speaker at the luncheon we decided to attend was the President's Press Secretary who delivered an entertaining speech about his first year on the job. He was young and enthusiastic and funny to listen to. While Ruth and I enjoyed his speech, we weren't there to get an insider's perspective of the White House. Over the years, thanks to our parents, Ruth and I have met more presidents in our lifetime than most people do in ten lifetimes. While the speaker was very engaging to listen to, I was aware of the fact that we were there for another reason. That reason was Harlan Ellis.

Ruth and I were seated at one of many large round tables spread around the spacious banquet hall. Despite my headache from the previous social event, I was hoping to share the table with Harlan. I wanted to sit next to him to hear every word he spoke in addressing the other people sharing our table. In the days leading up to the luncheon, I made a phone call and had the appropriate arrangements made to have our seats moved closer together. However, once we arrived, Ruth insisted we move our name cards to the opposite side of the table. Once seated, I quickly realized that decision made it a bit of a challenge for me to see Harlan's face thanks to six red roses popping up from a vase at the center of the table.

"You know, I can't see him very well," I complained, leaning to my left to look around the arrangement. "I don't know why I let you switch our name cards, sister. We were right beside him and then you made us move."

"You kept getting headaches," Ruth whispered back. "I just didn't want you sitting next to his whiny voice one more time. Besides, we're out of aspirin at home so you can't get any more headaches until we get to the store."

"Well, I did come prepared this time," I whispered, before fishing out a plastic baggie that contained the last aspirin from our home.

"I came prepared, too," Ruth grinned and she pointed to a cluster of people at the open bar. "I had a stiff drink before we sat down."

"A stiff drink?" I asked.

"I actually had two," Ruth giggled. "Another trip to the bar and I'm well on my way to forgetting everything I hear from that lapdog tonight!"

"Hush, sister," I scolded, glancing at the woman sitting beside Ruth. "Like I said, I only have one aspirin and I don't need *you* to give me a reason to use it tonight."

For the next few minutes, we sat at our table watching the guests arrive. We found ourselves nodding to a few familiar faces entering the hall and a few faces we knew who were taking their seats at our table. Then we finally saw Harlan arrive.

He wore a gray suit that was one shade darker than his hair. His eyes shifted from left to right, surveying each table that he walked by. He circled the room once, then finally returned to our table. The moment he sat down he looked around the centerpiece and smiled right at me. I was surprised at how quickly he picked us out from the other people sitting at our table.

"Hello again, Dupree sisters," he waved, straining his neck to look around the centerpiece. "We certainly do seem to be traveling in the same circles these days."

I thought about how best to respond to his observation.

"Perhaps you're following us, Harlan," I joked before offering a sly grin to underscore my clever comment.

"I agree," Ruth added, looking around the centerpiece at Harlan. "He *does* seem to be chasing after us quite a bit these days, don't you agree, sister?"

"Maybe he's smitten with us," I grinned.

Harlan smiled and his cheeks pushed back some of his wrinkles.

"I don't know about that," he said, pointing across the table, "but I do think I know why you two keep following *me* around."

I could feel my heart pop into my throat and I took a deep breath and tried to remain calm. He sounded very sure of himself and my mind was racing with what he was going to say next. I laced my fingers together and pulled my elbows up on the table.

"Do tell?" I calmly asked.

"For as long as I've known you two, you've always been a couple of curious ladies," Harlan began. "I think one...or both of you...must have become infatuated with my story about that murder I stumbled across at the National Portrait Gallery."

I quietly nodded my head thinking of how to respond.

"You might be right, Harlan," I casually stated. "You do seem to be talking about Webb Mills' death a good bit these days. Like you said, Ruth and I do enjoy a good mystery. I don't know about my sister but listening to your words is like watching a murder mystery unfold in my head."

"When I listen to you, Harlan, I find myself hanging on every detail," Ruth said with the kind of sarcastic tone that only a sister could pick up on.

"Well," Harlan said, a small smile melting across his lips, "I do hope I don't disappoint you two ladies this evening."

I offered a measured smile in reply while undoing my napkin and placing it on my lap.

My attention then turned to a lovely crystal goblet being placed in front of me by a server. It was teeming with lush blueberries, sliced mango and ripe red raspberries. While I ate, I let my eyes study the faces of the other guests sitting around me.

There were seven other people sharing our table. Sitting directly to my right was a middle-aged man named Spencer Wood, who told me he was the Chief Counsel of the IRS. A pleasant man, perhaps in his fifties, who quickly informed me that he was not promoted but appointed to his job by the President. Thus, given the stern and professional reputation of the IRS, I was pleasantly surprised to find Mr. Wood to be a charming conversationalist.

Because of his position with the Internal Revenue Service, Mr. Wood told me he was in charge of more than one thousand four hundred tax attorneys spread around the country. At first, he was tight lipped, which meant I had to offer warm smiles and easy topics to lure him out of his one and two word responses. I began by asking about his wife and children, then commented on his sense of humor before I decided to share some thoughts on private schools for said children. I even learned his mother and I had a fondness for the same mystery author. As the topics came and went, I could sense Mr. Wood's defenses melting away. His demeanor gradually warmed and he eventually began to engage me in conversation.

Whether it was the drinks he was consuming, or my relentless sunny nature, Mr. Wood opened up about his job in greater detail. This was especially true when talking about the various unusual reports that landed on his desk from people trying to avoid paying their fair share in taxes.

"I would imagine it is quite difficult to win every legal case that comes across your desk," I observed.

He nodded while taking a sip from his glass.

"As I learned fairly early in my work as an attorney," he proclaimed, "it's not in what they say or show you that's incriminating. It's what they hide or conceal. Never focus on the obvious when looking for the truth. Never just consider the evidence as someone presents it to you. Focus on the evidence that isn't readily visible to the eye. That's the trick when you investigate some tax cases. Don't consider what's in plain sight, Miss Dupree, but consider the things that are not readily visible."

After hearing those words, my eyes turned to Harlan, who was busy chatting to the person beside him. It was the same scene I'd been seeing over and over again for the last few weeks. The obvious scene. Then I turned back to Mr. Wood and thought about his words. That's when I began to realize I was focusing on the wrong source for information. Perhaps there was another way to learn the truth behind Webb Mills' death.

Chapter 23: The Surprise

Team of Rivals is one of my favorite books. It centers on the Presidency of Abraham Lincoln. Specifically, how Lincoln filled his cabinet with a wide range of personalities that were different from his own. I like the book because I admire Lincoln for not surrounding himself with "yes" men who gave him easy answers to complicated problems. He wanted debate and disagreement because he knew looking at a problem from different perspectives was the best way to formulate a quality solution.

Of course, many years have passed since President Lincoln's service. Yet, I can't help but notice how Washington remains a city with a fondness for simple answers to complex issues. Knowing this caused the face of Webb Mills to flash in my mind.

In the weeks after his death, it was clear to me that there was no simple solution to his murder. No obvious killer to accuse. Even the newspapers grew weary of following the case. This was evident to me when they stopped running stories about the investigation. From what Ruth and I could surmise through our social circles, the police were no longer questioning people who were in attendance at the gala. It appeared to us that the case had simply gone cold.

I pondered these thoughts one morning while lounging on the cream-colored couch in our sitting room, holding *Team of Rivals* on my lap. The morning light poured in through the windows, brightly illuminating the pages of my book. Yet, despite these perfect conditions (silence, bright light, a sharp mind) I found myself holding the book but not reading a word. The thoughts I harbored about Webb's death were simply too distracting to ignore.

I took a deep breath, stroked Oliver who was curled up on the couch beside me, and glanced out the window at the morning activity. From my vantage point, I saw two clear signs that it was a Monday morning. Cars were passing on the street in thicker patterns. Government workers packed the sidewalk in front of our house. My thoughts were interrupted when Ruth entered the room carrying a mug of hot tea. She settled into her favorite chair, the one facing the bay window with a perfect view of the street, and began to sip her tea. She looked around and smiled.

"How many people do you think have been entertained in this room over the years?" she asked.

I put *Team of Rivals* down on a side table and looked at her.

"Are you talking about *our* parties or *mother's* parties?" I asked.

"Both," Ruth said and she turned to look at me. "Of course, we haven't thrown as many parties as mother. In fact, we haven't even held a party in a long time."

"So true," I nodded.

"Perhaps we should have a party here over the holidays," Ruth suggested. "Trim the home with some tasteful decorations and invite our closest friends."

I grew silent for a moment, contemplating the idea. A truck rumbling down the street could faintly be heard through the window. I slowly stroked Oliver's soft fur again and turned to my sister.

"You know," I began, "I remember whenever mother was preparing to entertain guests she had a phrase she liked to use. It was about the quality of the food. Do you remember what she'd say?"

"Mother said lots of things before a party," Ruth replied, her eyes rolling like she did when she was fifteen. "I tried to ignore most of it when I was younger."

"Before entertaining, I remember how mother would be quite busy directing the maids and joining them in preparations," I recalled. "Then, every once in a while, I think father would feel guilty and offer to run to the market for some things. When he'd make that offer mother always would say, "If you want fresh meat, you don't go to the market…you go to the butcher." Do you remember that line?"

"That does sound familiar," Ruth nodded. "I always thought it was her dismissive way of not letting father pick out the food for her parties."

"Perhaps," I nodded. "I was reminded of that phrase last evening when I was having a lovely conversation with a gentleman from the IRS named Spencer Wood. What he said has led me to believe we've been chasing the wrong source for information about what happened to Webb."

"How so?" Ruth asked, her eyebrows lowering.

"Let's review our plan," I stated. "We've been after Harlan for weeks, listening to every scrap of information he drops. Thinking back on mother's words, and Mr. Wood's advice, it's caused me to re-examine our approach to this murder. It occurred to me that we've been following Harlan because we think he's the only good source of information about this case. After giving it a good deal of thought, I'm beginning to think there's another source we haven't been considering. A better source that we haven't tapped."

"Who?" Ruth asked.

I stood up from my comfy seat, grabbed a slip of paper and pencil and wrote down a name. When I handed the paper to my sister, she looked at the name, turned to me and grinned at my revelation. It was a source of information that, up to this point, neither one of us had considered tapping. A second source of information that, I thought, was long overdue for a conversation.

"Let's make a phone call," I suggested.

Ruth was one step ahead of me, already dialing a number she knew quite well.

Chapter 24: The Guest Arrives

The holiday season is a festive time in Washington. It really is a time go to parties and see friendly faces. That spirit clearly bit my sister, who rightfully suggested we throw a small party in our home. It had been a long time since we hosted one. Ruth and I talked for quite some time before deciding to arrange a small gathering. After some discussion, we decided a Saturday morning would be the best day of the week to hold our little get together. We also knew it would be quite different from the other parties we hosted during past holiday seasons.

For the rest of the week we laid out some plans. We discussed names, made phone calls and built up a list of individuals we felt would go well with the type of party we were thinking of hosting. Unlike the other parties we've held in the past, we quickly determined that this one would require very little preparation to throw. Most times when we'd host a social event in our home we'd spend a good deal of time on the details. We'd focus on preparing the food, fixing up the house, and reviewing topics of conversation we thought our friends would find engaging. However, nothing like that was required for this particular occasion. In fact, we knew for this particular event that we were about to break the first rule of hosting a party. We were about to make one of our guests very uncomfortable.

When Saturday morning arrived, it seemed strange not to be attending to details before our guest arrived.

There were no final touches to be made for catering, drinks, or even flower arrangements. This party simply required Ruth and me to stand in the foyer, wait for the doorbell and greet each guest as they entered our home. Most of our guests arrived on time. However, Ruth and I found ourselves waiting for one final guest to come. It was the most important guest. The reason for the gathering. Waiting for him to arrive was made even more nerve racking because he was late.

"Where is he?" Ruth mumbled, checking her watch. "I hope he's coming."

"He'll be here," I replied.

She stepped down the hall to peak in on our other guests, made a few comments, then returned to stand with me.

"He better show up," Ruth complained.

"He's coming," I coolly answered.

"How can you be so calm?" she asked, struggling to control the volume of her voice. "What makes you think he's not going to ignore our invitation?"

"When I invited him I spoke with him on the phone," I explained. "I lured him with the promise of fresh gossip. Like dangling a small bone in front of a hungry lapdog, sister. He'll be here eventually."

I stepped to the side of the door and peered out a small side window. From there I spotted a short narrow figure, wrapped in a dark winter coat, trudging down the snow-covered sidewalk with short brisk strides. When he drew closer I could make out Harlan's gray hair, and the sad expression that he always wore on his face. I saw him pause and step through the wrought iron gate that wrapped around our small property. Soon the doorbell rang and I slowly placed my hand on the door knob and turned it. I paused for a second, forced a smile on my face, and then cracked the door open wide.

"Good morning, Harlan," I smiled.

"And a chilly morning to you too, Charlotte," Harlan said, stepping into our parlor while rubbing his hands together. The moment he stepped into the foray his head tilted up, down, left and right to take in his surroundings. "So nice of you two ladies to invite me over. I don't think I've ever been here before. The hardwood floors look very nice."

"Thank you," Ruth said, holding out her hand. "Given the holiday season it seemed like a proper time to extend an invitation. May I take your things?"

"Thank you," he said, slipping off his coat and gloves before handing them to Ruth. "The hallway is charming. The décor here is lovely, ladies."

"Thank you," I replied.

His head turned to the left and the right, then he held his hand up to his ear.

"It's also very quiet in here," Harlan observed. He turned to me and his bushy white eye brows curled up like two little storm clouds. "I thought you said this was going to be a party, Charlotte? Shouldn't I be seeing some guests or hearing some voices? Am I early?"

"You're right on time," Ruth said, waving Harlan down the hallway. "Come right this way, Harlan. Step into our sitting room and warm up. The other guests are in there and they can't wait to hear your story."

Together Ruth and I led Harlan into our sitting room. Halfway down the hall he looked down at Oliver, who was stretched out on the hardwood floor, and I heard him mumble something about being allergic to cats. It was a comment I chose to ignore.

We led Harlan out of the hallway and into the sitting room. He stopped in his tracks the very second he stepped through the doorway.

I looked at him. His mouth clamped shut and I swear the color had drained from his face in seconds. His eyes slowly turned as he reviewed the face of every guest in the room. I can only guess how quickly his heart was racing. He stood, frozen at the entrance, just staring and taking in every detail before him.

Occupying most every chair and couch in our sitting room were the other guests. A mix of men and women of all ages who sat quietly and stared at Harlan. No one spoke. No one moved. I could sense the tension in the air. I knew every face in that room was a familiar one to Harlan. I also knew that they were faces he'd accused of committing murder.

Chapter 25: The Intervention

I glanced around the room and looked into the eyes of each of our guests. Directly to the right of where Harlan was standing was Representative Wendell Cremins. Knowing how fast he could walk and talk, Wendell looked quite at ease seated on one of our cream-colored chairs. Standing by the fireplace was Clayton Thompson, stroking his chin and squinting at Harlan. Clayton was good enough to take a break from running elections to accept our invitation to our little gathering. Seated on the couch petting one of our casts was Sydney Sterling, Webb's former personal assistant. Finally, sipping some coffee directly across from where Sydney was seated was none other than Daisy Mills herself. To come to our little party, Daisy managed to catch a flight back up from North Carolina. The one thing that surprised me was how happy she appeared to see Sydney in the same room. They even exchanged a brief hug and some chit-chat.

"What is all this?" Harlan finally asked, his squeaky voice rising going up by the end of the sentence.

Ruth turned and pulled two sliding doors shut to seal off the sitting room from the hall. I stepped up to Harlan and smiled.

"This is an intervention," I announced, trying to stare into his narrow beady eyes. "Let's just call it an intervention for the truth!"

"What do you mean...an intervention for truth?" Harlan asked.

"It means you should shut your mouth for once and listen to someone else speak," Ruth quickly advised.

"But..." he started to say.

"Let me explain the theme of this little party," I interrupted, gesturing with one hand to the other people in the room. "All of our guests who are present were kind enough to come because they have one thing in common. You see, Harlan, all of these people have been accused of killing Webb Mills...by you. As you know, Ruth and I have been attending the same parties as you these last few weeks. We've mingled with the same people you have. We've heard you offer the same details about Webb's murder to most every social engagement you attended."

"With a few minor changes for dramatic effect, of course," Ruth smirked.

"Now when I listened to your account at different parties I noticed how you would point suspicion at a different suspect at different events," I continued.

"You're confused, Charlotte," Harlan meekly objected.

"I have a very good memory," I continued, undeterred by his comment. "To the best of my recollection, you have identified a different suspect at every party you attended. In fact, you also offered a different motive for why Webb Mills was murdered. After overhearing so many accounts, I found your reasons for his murder to be less than reliable."

"Someone killed him," Harlan weakly offered.

"There may be a guilty party in this room," I nodded. "The last party I attended with you, I heard you use a very weak motive to accuse a very good friend of murder. The accusation made me angry, Harlan. Very angry. That's when I realized the only way to get to the truth was to gather all of your suspects in one room and confront each of them with your theories. So, Harlan, let's clear the air on some matters, shall we?"

Harlan glared at me like a garden gnome in a foul mood.

"Why don't we start with the widow, Daisy Mills," I began, walking over to Daisy who appeared very composed despite what she heard. "Shortly after Webb's death, Harlan began to implicate you in your husband's murder. I know this is a hard question for me to ask, but where were you when this crime took place, Daisy?"

"I was seated with the Director of the National Portrait Gallery," Daisy quietly replied. "The two of us were chatting about their newest exhibit when Webb excused himself to go to the restroom. I never left my seat when he was gone. And...I never spoke to my husband again."

Daisy stopped and shook her head, as if still absorbing the blow.

"Ruth and I had a lovely conversation with the director to verify your story," I nodded.

"The director was even nice enough to show Ruth and me security footage that showed Daisy in her seat chatting with the director. She never left the table. Such a shame that the cameras weren't installed in the men's bathroom, too. It would make this situation easier to resolve."

"And a bit more disgusting," Ruth mumbled.

"Disgusting...but helpful," I nodded.

"And what about you, Clayton?" Ruth asked, pointing across the room. "Did you know that Harlan also implied that you killed Webb for financial gain? He even claimed you were broke. Is your consulting business suffering that much?"

"Hardly!" Clayton snapped, his red face growing maroon and his eyes narrowing in Harlan's direction.

"I've known these ladies for many years. That's why I instructed my accountant to share my books with Charlotte and Ruth about a week ago. We met with my accountants who showed them quarterly statements for this year. As they can tell you, Harlan, I'm far from broke. This city has deep pockets. There was always enough of the pie for Webb and myself to divide. Neither one of us was going broke. On the contrary, I've had to turn away Webb's clients since his death because I'm so busy with my own clients."

My eyes turned to Harlan, who was staring at the floor.

"And what about that evening?" Ruth asked.

"I was with my wife the whole evening," Clayton quickly replied. "I know you two spoke with her and she confirmed it. We were together on the dance floor and at our table for dinner. Didn't leave the table once during dinner. The other people at our table can also confirm my story."

"Indeed," Ruth nodded. "I, for one, do remember seeing you two dancing together. Such genuine affection on display...it warmed my heart to watch you two sway to the music. Of course, the genuine love on your faces was quickly wiped away when Harlan stepped into the center of the dance floor to make his announcement."

I walked around to where our youngest guest was seated.

"This is Sydney Sterling," I continued and my eyes glanced in her direction. "She was also nice enough to accept our invitation to this party."

Sydney was enjoying a seat by the fireplace with her arms folded at her waist. She smiled when I said her name and nervously adjusted her platinum blond hair that fell over her shoulders. She turned and her blue eyes narrowed in the direction of Harlan.

"What did he say about me?" Sydney softly asked.

"It seems Harlan has been telling people about your affair with Webb," I stated.

Sydney's face went from a natural pale tone to bright red. Her eyes grew wider and they darted around to the other faces in the room before returning to Harlan.

"Lies," she quietly hissed at Harlan.

I glanced at Daisy out of the corner of my eye and there was no emotion on her face, which I found rather surprising.

"Now, Sydney, you were nice enough to provide phone records to us the night Webb died," Ruth stated.

"That's right," Sydney nodded.

"We looked at the records with you," I continued. "They showed you were on your phone at the time that Webb was murdered. It was so nice of you to contact your phone provider to send you the log of your phone calls that evening. I called one number that the log indicated was dialed at the time of Webb's death. It was, as you told me, your mother who was speaking with you right around the time Harlan came out of the bathroom. I would think it's hard to strangle someone with one hand while the other is holding a phone. Don't you agree, sister?"

"Absolutely," Ruth smiled, turning to yet another guest. "And as for Wendell? Well, he was speaking with Clayton Thompson for most of the evening. From what we were told, Wendell's wife told me he was trying to convince Clayton to run his re-election campaign. Of course, as Clayton told us, it made for a long evening of listening to Wendell ramble on about his various notions on why Clayton should run the campaign and how they would both benefit."

"I only made a *few* suggestions," I heard Wendell mumble. "It's not a crime to try to recruit the best in the business."

I noticed how Clayton smiled at Wendell's words. I took some steps towards Harlan. I looked around to find every face in the room focused on me. I cleared my throat and stopped in front of Harlan.

"As you can see, Harlan," I smiled and gestured around the room to our guests. "Everyone in this room was minding their own business that evening. Everyone has someone who will testify that they were not anywhere near the bathroom committing a murder. And yet, you still insist on dragging these people, and their good names, through the mud. Why?"

Chapter 26: Truth

Harlan looked around the room. His eyes began to blink very quickly, perhaps reflecting how fast his brain cells were formulating an answer to Daisy's news. He sat down on a cream-colored loveseat, nervously crossed one leg and turned his eyes to the floor. I was very curious to hear the first words that would come out of his mouth.

"When I went to the bathroom that night…the lights were low…and I just wasn't paying attention to who was coming out of the bathroom when they knocked into me," he stated at a hint above a whisper. "You know it's funny how a memory can change. Some days, I thought it was a man…some days a woman."

"Harlan!" Ruth objected in a shrill voice. She paused and let a little grin fill her face. "I swear if you can't tell the difference between a man and a woman then your mother did a horrible job of raising you."

I couldn't help but smile at my sister's humorous jab.

"The truth!" Ruth snapped.

Harlan closed his mouth and said nothing.

I walked across the room and pointed to another guest.

"Now our good friend, Daisy Mills, has flown all the way up from North Carolina for this little event," I explained. "Do you know why?"

"No," Harlan answered, his eyes blinking quickly.

"Closure," I replied, staring at Harlan.

His eyes didn't blink once, but he started to bite his bottom lip.

"You see, Daisy called us just a few days ago," I began. "It seems the police contacted her with some news about her husband's case. News that she wanted to share with us."

"Daisy," Ruth jumped in. "Please tell our guests what you told us."

"Very well," Daisy Mills spoke up, standing up from her chair. She stepped to the center of the room and cleared her throat. "Since I flew back to North Carolina to bury my husband, I hadn't heard any news from the police. Weeks flew by and still not one phone call. Then, a few days ago, the police finally contacted me with some very surprising news. You see, when Webb died the police conducted an autopsy. It took them a while but they finally called me with the results. What they told me was so surprising it led me to board a plane and fly up here for this little party."

"And what was their news?" I asked.

Daisy turned and looked at every face in the room.

"They told me the truth," Daisy replied, and her eyes stopped and locked on Harlan. "After conducting their autopsy, I know the truth about what happened to my husband. You see, they told me that Webb died of a heart attack....and nothing more."

The mood in the room changed. The expressions on the faces grew different. This was no longer a gathering for our guests to express their anger with Harlan. They were no longer casually seated waiting their turn to take a shot at Harlan for accusing them of murder. Instead they were all focused on Daisy and her surprising news.

"Did you say he *wasn't* murdered?" Wendell finally asked, leaning forward in his seat.

"I asked the police about the accusation of murder," Daisy reported. "They told me...there was no murder."

"But what about the rope around your husband's neck?" Sydney spoke up. "Wasn't that a big enough clue to suggest he was strangled?"

"He wasn't strangled," Daisy replied. "When they performed the autopsy, which is how they determined the heart attack, the coroner also found that the rope around his neck left no bruises on the skin. This, or so the coroner said, indicated that Webb wasn't strangled to death. He simply died from a massive heart attack."

"But Harlan," I said, turning to our guest of honor, "you were the one who told the police you found Webb with a rope around his neck. What do you make of this news?"

"I didn't read anything in the newspapers about a heart attack," Harlan grumbled, still nervously fidgeting with his hands.

"Are you calling me a liar, Harlan?" Daisy asked, her voice remaining surprisingly calm while she spoke.

Harlan's mouth dropped open a crack but no words came out.

"Out of respect for our family," Daisy continued, "I asked the police to keep these details under wraps. When I spoke to Ruth and Charlotte and they told me what you've been doing, Harlan, I knew I wanted to confront you about those rumors you've been spreading. That's why I flew back here. So, tell me, Harlan, why *have* you been running around this town screaming murder from one party to the next? Why have you been insisting this is a murder when, in fact, it wasn't?"

The question lingered in the air without a response. It appeared to me that Harlan was holding his tongue and formulating his words carefully. Only the ticking sound of our beloved grandfather clock filled the room. Harlan turned an angry eye towards me, if only for a few seconds, and I could sense his exasperation for being tricked into coming to our little gathering. I maintained eye contact with him and refused to look away.

"Harlan," I began, "you can rest assured that we didn't invite any police officers to our home for this modest affair. We did that for a reason."

"As we stated when you arrived," Ruth jumped in. "This is an intervention for truth. That's why we never considered putting the police on our list of guests."

"Now, Harlan, we are all here for nothing more than the truth," I nodded. "So tell us again how you found Webb's body and when you decided to deem it a murder? Tell us when you decided it would be a good idea to spread a lie and stir the pot with gossip. I think Daisy is entitled to that."

Harlan remained silent, still staring at me while his face was flushed.

"Why did you decide to ruin the name of Webb Mills?" Ruth chimed in.

Again, Harlan remained silent.

"But that person who knocked me down," Harlan weakly began and his eyebrows went up to form an all too familiar expression of innocence. "The killer leaving the bathroom just ran right over me."

"As I said," Ruth interrupted, raising her voice to a louder, sharper level than I was used to hearing. "This is an intervention for truth! I've listened to you for weeks, Harlan! I know every version of your lies. You must be honest with us, or we *will* call the police right now. Poor Daisy came all the way up from North Carolina to share the truth about how her husband died. Give her some closure. Now tell us the what happened that night or, so help me God, my next call will be to 911 asking for the police to send their best officer to our home."

I could tell by the expression on his face that Harlan was none too pleased with Ruth's request. His face glistened with sweat and a slight smile curled under his cheeks.

"No," he mumbled.

"So you would prefer the police to be here?" I asked.

"Go ahead and call them," Harlan snapped, glancing at me. "I'll tell them the same thing I said at the gala. It makes no difference to me."

At this point I didn't think we'd get Harlan to admit to anything. Then, my sister stepped across the room and grabbed Harlan by his arm.

"Wait, Ruth," I said, sensing she was letting her emotions get the better of her.

"I'm fine," she assured me in a calmer voice. "I simply want to talk to Harlan, alone, in the hallway."

Ruth got a firm grip on his arm and pulled him right out of his seat with more strength than I thought she had. Harlan's mouth dropped open, perhaps surprised by the force my sister used to jerk him to his feet. His eyes squinted together as she pulled him out of the sitting room and into the hallway.

"You're not being a good host!" his meek voice echoed from the hall.

"Stay out here and listen to what I have to say because I'm only going to say it once," Ruth stated in a firm voice.

I stayed in the room with our other guests waiting for Harlan and Ruth to return. Silence filled the moment, leaving me to smile at my guests while they turned their gaze between me and the hallway. For a few seconds, I began to wonder if they were even in the hallway or if they stepped outside.

"What is she up to?" I whispered to myself.

Curiosity got the better of me. I stepped into the hallway where I found Ruth and Harlan standing by the front door, speaking almost nose to nose. I watched how Ruth leaned into him and whispered something in his ear. He took one step back from her, looking as if she had just punched him in the stomach. He covered his mouth with his hand. The look of shock on his face told me whatever she said really surprised him. He went to say something in reply but Ruth quickly put her index finger up in the air and pointed back into the sitting room. Like an obedient dog, Harlan slowly turned, glanced at Ruth one more time, then took a few steps back into the sitting room. I trailed behind them, wishing I knew what Ruth had said to change Harlan's mind. When I entered the sitting room, I looked around at our guests. They were all staring at Harlan. He stepped to the center of the room, cleared his throat and parted his lips.

"We want the truth!" Ruth demanded.

"The truth?" Harlan asked.

Ruth and I both nodded.

Harlan looked around. The whole room was silent. All eyes turned to our guest. We watched as Harlan nervously tucked his hands in his trouser pockets, parted his lips and began to share what really happened on that fateful night at the National Portrait Gallery's Gala.

For the first time in weeks, it struck me that I wasn't hearing the same old narrative. From the tone of his voice to the way he sat, it seemed to me that I was listening to a different version of Harlan Ellis. A version I'd never experienced before. For the first time in weeks, I felt like what I was hearing were honest words and not dramatized fiction. It made for an intriguing couple of moments.

Chapter 27: Harlan's Story

"I have a niece," Harlan began. "Her first name is Mia. No last names for this story. All I'll say about Mia is that she's the sweetest woman I know. Her heart is as pure as Eve before the apple. Ever since she was a little girl she always wanted to be a teacher. The classroom was always where her passion resided. When she graduated from college she got a job as a high school social studies teacher in her hometown of Florence, Virginia. For as long as I've known her, Mia always wanted to be a teacher. A few years ago, Mia decided to try something different. She felt inspired to run for a retiring representative's seat in her district. She tossed her hat in the ring and chose to campaign for the vacant seat."

"Why did she decide to go from teaching to politics?" I asked.

"At first, her students urged her to do it after a lesson," Harlan explained. "She said 'no' but they kept after her. When she decided to run, it was to show her students that public service was important for everyone to do, no matter how rich or poor."

"A noble lesson to demonstrate," I nodded.

"Of course," Harlan continued, "once she began campaigning this lesson turned into something much bigger. You see, my niece cares very deeply about women's rights and she thought she could make a difference if elected. Webb Mills was running the campaign for the opposing candidate. I was concerned about what he might do to my niece. As you many know, I never married so I don't have children of my own. My dear Mia has always been like a daughter to me. She's a tough young woman with a thick skin…but when she dipped her toe into political waters she had no idea what was about to happen to her."

"And what was that?" I asked.

"Running against a campaign being orchestrated by Webb Mills," Harlan replied and he took a deep breath before shaking his head at what he was seeing in his head. "In the beginning, it was fun for Mia. She went around to county fairs and marched in parades and shook hands and made a few speeches. Like I said, it was fun."

Harlan paused and took another deep breath.

"I'm sure Webb kept one eye on the polls," he continued. "As the weeks went by, it appeared that Mia was keeping the race close. Gradually, I began to see some signs in yards or on billboards for Webb's candidate. When the election came down the home stretch, and the polls were still very close, that's when Webb came out swinging."

"How so?" I asked.

"He began to run TV ads against Mia," Harlan nodded. "At first, it was very innocent. People on the street saying nice things about Webb's candidate. But as they got closer to election day, I was surprised at how my niece was able to keep the race so tight. I think Webb was also surprised. Two weeks before the election, that's when he decided to get dirty for his candidate."

"What do you mean by dirty?" Ruth asked.

"He made an ad about Mia's support of woman's rights for birth control," Harlan explained. "The narrative of the ad described how Mia was single and it made her sound like she was for birth control because she wasn't married and dated a lot of men. The ad implied she liked to sleep around...which was far from the truth! That just wasn't in Mia's character but it didn't stop Webb from telling that lie over and over."

"Oh dear," Ruth sighed.

"And how did Mia respond to these attack ads?" I asked.

"Of course, she was horrified by the accusations," Harlan continued. "The more she spoke to the press and objected to the lies, the more her opponent hinted that she had something to hide. She went on to lose the election but, more importantly, she lost her good reputation with the community."

"Such a shame," Ruth sighed.

"Shortly after the election, Mia was fired from her teaching job because of those lies," Harlan continued. "In fact, she couldn't find any school in the state that would hire her because of what people thought, thanks to Webb Mills. Eventually, she had to move out of state to find a teaching job. Because she had to relocate, well, let's just say I don't see much of my sweet Mia anymore. She lives in Kansas now. A thousand miles away from me all because of Webb Mills and his dirty ad."

I glanced over to Daisy, who was looking at her hands folded on her lap.

"I'm sorry, Harlan," I finally offered.

"Poor, Mia," Ruth spoke at just above a whisper.

"You know, I never forgave Webb for what he did," Harlan explained, settling into one of our cream-colored chairs. "So when I walked into that bathroom at that gala, and saw the mighty Webb Mills on the floor with his pants down to his knees, it seemed like the perfect opportunity to soil *his* reputation the way he soiled poor Mia's reputation. I wanted to do something to drag his name through the muck."

Harlan paused for a moment, looked out the bay window, and slowly nodded at the memory.

"I was alone in the room with Webb's body," he continued. "I heard a voice in the hall so I quickly turned and locked the bathroom door to keep everyone out. I knew most of the guests were eating dinner but I had to be careful. I thought I had maybe a minute at the most to think about what to do. That's when I noticed the maintenance closet in the bathroom. The door to the closet was open just a crack. I flung open the closet door and dug around and that's when I spotted the rope. I grabbed it from the closet, walked back to the bathroom stall and wrapped that rope around Webb's neck. I stood there for a second, then ran out of the bathroom and cried murder!"

"How could you?" Daisy hissed from her seat.

Harlan's eyes remained fixed on the bay window and he slowly shook his head.

"For everything your husband did to my niece," Harlan shrugged. "It just seemed like due justice to me. It still does."

No one spoke when Harlan was finished. There was nothing to say. The truth had put everyone's minds to rest and, for Daisy Mills, provided some closure to her husband's untimely demise. For everyone in the room, it was a reminder of how passionate politics can be. How powerful people who make a career in politics can impact the lives of average people. How Webb Mills did just that by forcing Harlan's niece out of the state of Virginia with one lie. How that same lie led Harlan to tarnish Webb's reputation by attending every social event he could to spread a rumor of murder. It was a lesson I will never forget.

Chapter 28: Resolution

"That's a remarkable story," Ian Walsh said, leaning back in his seat and stretching his arms high in the air. He turned to Ruth. "So what did you whisper to Harlan to force him to spill the beans? You must have really been rough with him."

"Me?" Ruth grinned, pointing to herself. "Oh, I promised Harlan fresh gossip and that's exactly what I gave him. I told him about a little piece of gossip I heard regarding a dalliance he had with a young man who works on a certain senator's staff. Harlan is old enough to be the boy's grandfather, but from what I heard, that didn't stop him from pursuing such a handsome young man. I told Harlan I'd be happy, more than happy, to share that gossip with the rest of Washington."

The moment Ian grinned at Ruth's words, Mezzo hopped on the couch next to him and climbed on his lap. Ian instinctively began to stroke the cat's back. Much to Charlotte's surprise, Mezzo appeared to be perfectly content sitting with their guest.

"Is what you told him the truth?" Ian asked.

"It's a rumor," Ruth sighed. "My experience with rumors is that they can be used for slander or for motivation. In Harlan's case, I chose the latter."

Ian quietly nodded at Ruth's explanation.

"So now you know the reason," Charlotte nodded to her guest.

"Beg your pardon? What reason?" Ian answered, leaning forward in his seat.

"You know," Charlotte continued. "The reason you stopped in today. The reason why your review was dropped. It was unfortunate for you that Harlan Ellis chose to do this at the gala. His actions were just enough to bump your fine meal from the newspapers. I'm so sorry that happened, Ian. As I said before, at least you know why."

"After listening to that story...I forgot all about the review," Ian laughed, shifting in his seat while he continued to pet Oliver. "I guess that's why I came here, isn't it?"

"So you told us," Ruth nodded.

"After hearing all the details of the story," Ian began, "I guess that review just doesn't seem all that important to me anymore. What that man, Harlan Ellis, did was unforgiveable. Did you ever report this story to the police? The newspapers? Someone?"

"Of course," Ruth answered with a sly grin. "It was interesting to find out that Harlan thought he wasn't breaking any laws by slipping that rope around Webb's neck. After all, Harlan reasoned, the body was already dead. However, slipping that rope around his neck did turn out to be a crime. Tampering with a corpse is a felony in this state, or so we learned."

"And then to accuse many innocent people of murder," Charlotte added. "Now that's the part of the story that *should* be a crime, in my opinion."

"So did anything happen to him?" Ian asked, his large round eyes growing narrow for the first time. "Was there some kind of punishment for what he did to all those people? The widow? The personal assistant? The campaign manager who knew Webb Mills? I think all of those people Harlan got into trouble by implying they committed murder would have liked to have seen some justice be done to him."

"Because he had no criminal record," Charlotte explained, "he was given probation and a hefty fine. However, from what I've been told, the more severe punishment is what Harlan has experienced since all this reached the social circles of Washington."

"Well, I know he didn't go to jail," Ian reported. "In fact, I just saw him in a restaurant I was working in last week."

"And what was he doing when you saw him?" Ruth asked.

"He was having lunch," Ian replied.

"Was he with anyone?" Charlotte asked.

"No, he was eating alone," Ian recalled.

Ruth and Charlotte looked at each other and smiled.

"And there's the punishment," Ruth nodded.

"What do you mean?" Ian asked, head turning from one sister to the other. "I...I don't understand. He still has his freedom. He can still go where he wants."

"Let me explain something, Ian," Charlotte began. "The social circles here in Washington can be...a fickle lot. It's like a club made up of powerful people who have been together for many, many years. We're like...a family. And so, when a member of the family gets hurt...the rest of the family responds in kind."

"I'm still not following you," Ian confessed.

"You were right to say what you did about Harlan," Charlotte nodded. "He did hurt a lot of people in this town. And now, the social circles of Washington D.C. have responded in kind to what he did."

"How?" Ian asked.

Charlotte smiled at the question. Sometimes she forgot she was addressing not just a gifted chef, but also a very young man.

"Let's just say my sister and I no longer have to listen to Harlan speak at any social functions," Charlotte explained.

"In fact, we don't even have to see that little lapdog at any parties or fundraisers, too," Ruth added.

"That's true," Charlotte pointed to Ruth. "Harlan is just not as visible as he used to be."

"Invisible is a better word," Ruth grinned.

"Why?" Ian asked.

"Because no one will invite him anymore," Ruth chimed in.

"Or so we've been told," Charlotte added.

"From what I hear about our little friend," Ruth grinned, "he's leading a very solitary life these days. No one answers his phone calls. No one invites him to social events. The social circles of Washington have been closed off to Harlan. I would imagine that he pretty much sits at home, alone, holding his phone waiting for someone to ask him to attend a party, or luncheon, or even a tea. What Harlan might not realize is that the invitation he's waiting for...it just won't be coming."

"So that's his punishment?" Ian asked. "Just that? He'll be drinking tea alone?"

"I know it may not sound like very much to you," Charlotte explained, "but for Harlan...exile is the greatest punishment. No more audiences to listen to him speak. No more people to stroke his ego with special treatment. And if he *does* tell a story, it will always be taken with a grain of salt. The rest of Washington society now knows what my sister and I have known for years: the simple fact that Harlan Ellis is a liar."

"He also got a hefty fine from a judge," Ruth eagerly reported.

With that final statement, Ian quietly nodded and looked around the room.

"Your sister said there's a football game on," Ian said, checking his watch. "Do you think we still have time to watch the end of it?"

"After everything we told you…why would you be interested in football?" Charlotte asked.

"I like the team," Ian shrugged. "Besides, after hearing that story, I guess I'm hoping for at least one happy ending today. Maybe it'll happen on a football field."

Charlotte turned to Ruth who had a broad smile on her face and gave her a nod.

"There might be some time left," Ruth quickly stated, grabbing the remote and turning on the TV.

With a green screen in front of them, the sound of cheers filling the air, Ruth smiled at the welcome sight. The score appeared at the bottom of the screen and it revealed that Washington was winning by one point with a few minutes left in the game.

"Here," Ruth said, shoving the old football in Ian's hands.

"What do you want me to do with this?" Ian asked.

"Just rub it for good luck," Ruth instructed.

"Ruth and I always rub it before the start of a game," Charlotte explained, squinting at the score on the screen. "Today, it looks like we need one more fan to rub it for extra luck."

Ian moved from the chair to the couch next to Ruth and quickly did as he was instructed. Charlotte smiled at her sister and her guest, both leaning forward, both with their mouths hanging open, both staring at the screen. Then Ruth blinked once and looked over to see Charlotte grinning.

"What?" Ruth asked, pointing at the TV.

"Don't look so worried, sister," Charlotte answered, shaking her head. "You know that there's always a happy ending right around the corner."

Ruth quickly turned her eyes back to the screen, unaware of the fact that when speaking of happy endings Charlotte was not talking about the football game.

Even though the holiday spirit was on full display in Washington, Ruth and Charlotte just hadn't been feeling very festive for the last couple of weeks. Despite the lights, the music, and the symbols of the season filling the city, the Dupree sisters just weren't in a celebratory mood. Given the death of Webb and the departure of Daisy, it was difficult to muster any feelings to celebrate the season.

One evening, they talked and decided to put up some holiday decorations around the house in an attempt to usher the holiday spirit into their hearts. It was on this evening that their decorating was interrupted by a knock on the door. Charlotte stepped down the hallway and opened the door. What she saw caused three words to slip out of her mouth.

"A Christmas miracle."

Standing on their porch was a familiar face that, like the flowers and the cherry blossoms, had vanished over the winter. A friend who had returned to Washington and, in less than a second, renewed the Dupree sisters' spirits.

"Daisy Mills!" Charlotte laughed. "What are you doing back in town?"

Suddenly, the sound of shoes smacking on hardwood floors could be heard. Charlotte turned to see Ruth quickly approaching from the kitchen. She stepped by me and out to the front stoop before wrapping her arms around Daisy. Together they stood, in the crisp December air, neither one appearing to be cold.

"I knew you couldn't stay away," Ruth grinned before stepping back and looking at Daisy. "How long are you here for this time?"

"I'm moving back into my home here in Washington," Daisy smiled, glancing at Ruth and Charlotte.

"I thought you were going to stay in North Carolina with Webb?" Charlotte asked, taking one step out of her home onto the front porch. "Did you just arrive from the airport?"

"I've been back in my home for about a week," Daisy replied.

"A week?" Ruth asked.

"What brings you back?" Charlotte said, her grin growing wider. "Have you spent the week packing the rest of your things? Tying up loose ends with the realtor?"

"No," Daisy sighed, tucking her hands into a black mink sable. "I...I tried to stay in North Carolina, ladies. Webb and I have a lovely home down there. But the days were just too quiet without him. I found myself visiting Webb's grave almost every day. I thought that going back to North Carolina would be a new start for me. But after a few months, I began to realize that I was staying there to accompany my husband's body...not to be close to his spirit."

She took a deep breath, rewrapped a gray scarf she was wearing around her neck and smiled at Daisy and Charlotte.

"I guess I learned something about myself in the last few months," Daisy continued. "I learned that I feel closer to Webb here...in Washington...even though his body is in North Carolina. This city...this is where I feel his spirit. I can sense him when I'm walking in Lafayette Square. I can feel him at the Old Ebbits Grille when I dine there. I think of him when I'm at a party and I hear guests discussing the newest candidates and how various elections are shaping up. To be honest, I've found more comfort here than I did in North Carolina. I know he's buried down south but there's a part of him that fills this city. That's why I'm back here, ladies. That's why I've decided to stay in Washington."

The words were so perfect that Ruth and Charlotte didn't know what to say. After a moment, Charlotte glanced at her watch.

"Well, we shouldn't keep you out on our front porch on such a chilly evening. Please come in and chat with us, Daisy," I suggested.

"Yes, come inside and tell us about those lovely grandchildren," Ruth stated, taking Daisy by the hand. "Later, we can get you caught up on all the gossip that you've missed."

Daisy nodded but she wasn't smiling. Instead, her face framed an expression of urgency.

"That sounds lovely," she nodded, "but first, I need to ask you two for a favor."

"And what would that be?" Ruth asked.

"I need you to come with me," Daisy replied while gesturing to a taxi idling by the curb.

It was a chilly evening and Charlotte instinctively wrapped her arms around her chest after hearing Daisy's request. She was ready to stay in her warm house for the night. Given the choice, she could sense that Ruth felt the same way on this dark December evening.

"Wouldn't you rather come inside?" Ruth asked again, trying to sweeten her invitation with a smile.

"Yes," Charlotte nodded. "I'll make some tea, or hot chocolate, or whatever you'd like."

Daisy looked none too happy with either sister's suggestions.

"Please come with me," Daisy begged. "You see, ladies, there's somewhere I need to go. It's a special place that Webb liked and…I'm afraid I'm just not strong enough to go there by myself. I could really use your support this evening. Please, come with me."

Without hesitation, Ruth and Charlotte stepped inside, grabbed their coats and followed Daisy down the steps from their front stoop and into a waiting taxi. Once inside the cab they were quickly whisked away into the night.

Lights flickered by the windows. The sound of Bing Crosby singing *White Christmas* played over the taxi's radio. Daisy stared out the window and didn't say a word about where they were going. Ruth and Charlotte had no idea what their final destination would be. They simply trusted in the fact that their friend needed them, which is why they were sharing the ride. Eventually, the cab slowed in front of a place that Ruth and Charlotte quickly recognized.

Framed in the window of the taxi, the U.S. Capital Building was illuminated in its pure white splendor. In the foreground, the Capital Christmas Tree was easily visible, adorned in its brightly glowing holiday lights. The taxi continued to follow the road, moving past the Capital Christmas Tree before stopping at an oddly shaped building that appeared to be made of glass. In the darkness, it was easy to see that the building held a soft glow to it. The structure wasn't as bright as the Capital Christmas Tree, but it was illuminated enough to remind travelers of its presence during the holiday season.

"The Botanic Gardens?" Ruth asked, turning to Daisy.

Daisy quietly nodded.

Both of them knew that the United States Botanic Garden is a lovely place to visit during the holiday season. Located on the grounds of the United States Capital, the structure is mainly a large glass greenhouse. The signature feature of the greenhouse is its rounded dome at the center of the building. The image is reminiscent of a snow globe filled with glowing colors and festive spirits. Following Daisy out of the cab, it was clear to Ruth and Charlotte that the festive spirits of the garden must have been a favorite of Webb's. Perhaps that was why Daisy needed them to join her on this cold winter night.

"Follow me," Daisy said, leading them from the street and through the main entrance.

They trailed behind Daisy as she entered the greenhouse. Once inside, all three of them were drawn to the festive lighting around the gardens. As they began to walk around, they quickly noticed a variety of train displays set up throughout the interior of the greenhouse.

"It's like stepping into a child's dream," Charlotte remarked to herself as she watched two little boys lingering next to one train display, pointing and grinning at every detail.

Aside from the trains, there were other things to admire. Small models of the White House and the Capital Building were on exhibit, along with sculptures of holiday symbols. They noted how every display was built from natural materials, which gave most visitors time to pause and appreciate the details. Sticks, flowers, hollowed-out logs and poinsettias were just some of the items used for constructing the scenes that, on this night, drew attention and praise from a steady stream of visitors.

"Oh, how Webb would have loved coming here during the holidays," Daisy beamed, her eyes dancing from one train display to the next. "He was an electric train enthusiast. It was a hobby he shared with the grandchildren. This place was just so magical for Webb. It transformed him from the man I loved to a little boy the moment we stepped in here."

"Really?" Charlotte asked, a little surprised by this revelation. "I find it hard to imagine Webb being anything but all-business."

"Oh, he was a teddy bear," Daisy grinned and she quietly nodded at one of the train displays. "How he loved the holiday season. Of course, he was very generous with the children and the grandchildren when it came to Christmas. Aside from politics, family was the other thing that Webb was passionate about."

The comment caused Ruth's head to whip towards Daisy. Her eyebrows lowered.

Charlotte stepped closer, recognizing the sign that Ruth had a thought that was about to pop out of her mouth.

"I have one question," Ruth began, making eye contact with Daisy. "We spoke to someone who confirmed that Webb and his personal assistant were…close. To be honest, this friend of mine observed them holding hands at a quiet restaurant in Georgetown. Now, at least Webb was subtle. He had rented out a private room in the restaurant and was sitting alone with this Sydney Sterling behind closed doors. In fact, my friend just happened to peek in when the waiter opened the door to serve them their meal. That's when she caught a glimpse of him holding her hand. Now…do I believe my friend? Absolutely. After hearing what you just said, it made me think back to our little party for Harlan. You were so cordial and gracious to Sydney. Were you even aware of Webb's indiscretion?"

Daisy quietly stepped to another train display. She stared at the scene before her and then drew in her breath.

"You know, the day I married Webb," she began, "I knew he had a lot of good qualities. I also knew he had one bad one; his fondness for flirting. As Webb grew in stature in this town, he became the center of many women's attentions. I quickly realized this would be a problem.

So one night we sat down and had a discussion. I told him I wasn't going to build a fence around him. I knew he loved our family, but I also knew he was fond of flirting. So we came to an arrangement. We agreed that flirting would be permissible, but nothing more. I also told him if he ever engaged in...intimacies with another woman...I would leave him in a heartbeat. I told him I would take our children and go back to North Carolina and hire the most expensive divorce attorney around. That was enough of a threat for him. So, yes, I'm sure he was holding her hand and smiling the way he does, but if you asked Sydney if she ever exchanged intimacies with my husband, she'd say 'no'."

"You're a strong woman, Daisy," Charlotte observed.

"You're only realizing that now?" Daisy grinned.

With those last words, Daisy quietly tucked her hands in her coat pockets and led them around the Botanical Gardens. They commented on a few more displays. They smiled at a few children enthusiastically pulling their parents around. They pointed at a few more interesting details and then they left. Daisy had instructed the taxi to wait for them while they toured the holiday displays.

As they slipped into the cold dark night, Charlotte turned and looked back at the greenhouse. She noted how it appeared to draw people in as a source of warmth and beauty, how it seemed to provide a light for people in the dark and bitter cold, how it appeared that visitors came because they knew inside they would find great beauty and warmth. She couldn't help but think of Daisy when she looked at the scene.

In a city filled with people who were too caught up in winning the next election, or passing the next bill, Daisy was simply a light. A pure light of love that both Ruth and Charlotte couldn't help but be drawn to. Friends such as Daisy were the best kind to have. The ones focused on what was in their hearts and not what was next on their path to power.

THE END

ABOUT THE AUTHOR

Allen B. Boyer is the author of two Young Adult novels and one nonfiction book about the West Point Academy and its famous graduates. His books have been sold around the country. His Bess Bullock Retirement Home Mystery series produced five books for Cozy Cat Press. *Death at the Presidents Church* began his new Dupree Sisters Mystery series. This book is the third in that series.

Mr. Boyer lives near Hershey, Pennsylvania, with his wife, Suzanne, and their three children. He likes to take his children and their dog to visit residents at a nearby retirement home.

www.ingramcontent.com/pod-product-compliance
Lightning Source LLC
Chambersburg PA
CBHW030255270626
47156CB00022B/2763